# Jungle Beauty Goddess's Pretty Blue Ball

Cassandra George-Sturges

Email Junglebeautygoddess@gmail.com

Independently published: **ISBN:** 9781707064281

# ABOUT THE AUTHOR

I dragged God behind me kicking and screaming, begging Him to help me accomplish every desire of my heart with the exception of the creations of Jungle Beauty Goddesses. "God, oh please let them accept me into the doctorate program; oh God please, let this class be open; oh God please help me to write this book and let it be a number one seller; Oh God please, please, please let me get this job…" and the list goes on. I have two master degrees, a doctorate in psychology, and have been teaching full-time for 10 years. I worked in the human services field for 13-years, and I have written five books.

But…sewing is the only endeavor in my life thus far where God is flowing through me; ideas are coming to me. I am saying, "Slow down God I can't sew that fast!" I decided to sew my first doll on a whim at forty-four. My family and friends thought that this was the funniest idea that they had ever heard. I sewed my first four dolls completely by hand. My boyfriend gave me a sewing machine for Christmas, but I had to take a class to learn how to use it.

Everyone told me that I should make my dolls smaller so that people could place them in their homes. I tried desperately to make them smaller, but the Universe created me with big hands with long thick fingers like my daddy. My hands are as big as or bigger than most men. Not only did I find making smaller dolls difficult and tedious, they were not attractive to me and did not resonate with my spirit. I concluded that if God had wanted me to make smaller dolls He would have given me smaller fingers.

Each Jungle Beauty Goddess is 60 inches / 5 ft. tall or taller. She is as exotically beautiful with her clothes on as in the nude. Her skin is made of suede cloth, she is filled with fiber, and depending on the JBG cloth doll sculpture her hair is weaved into her scalp. Her eyes are individually painted. She is believed to come to life the moment her eyes are secured into her sockets.

JBG noses are sculpted; lips are full, shapely, mini satin-like pillows. They have salon eyelashes, hand-painted imitation pearl eyeballs, and artificial nails on their fingers and toes. They can bend their elbows and knees to be placed in various sitting positions. The JBG's cannot stand alone.

Their voluptuous breasts have faux leather areolas and cotton nipples. Their genitalia includes pubic hair, the labia majora, the labia minora, and a gemstone clitoris that sits under the clitoral hood. Their buttocks are round, full, and shapely; they have small waists and protruding navels. JBG's are by no means sex dolls or meant to be used sexually. The JBG are not toys and are not designed for or safe for children to play with. These are life-size fabric sculptures that celebrate the femininity, power, and beauty of the human female form.

When I stopped listening to other people and just listened to the quiet voice inside of me, these Jungle Beauty Goddesses emerged from my dreams. While driving to work, I would see them gracefully running through the forest trees. I could feel the earth tremble each time their feet touched the ground. I wondered to myself whether or not I had gone completely and totally insane.

The Jungle Beauty Goddesses, Qattara, Kalahari, Sahara, Sinai, Chalbi, and Namib lived in my vivid imagination months before I could manifest their physical presentation. While sewing each JBG, I did not know that they were characters in a story. The entire story came to me in a dream from beginning to end.

I am Cassandra George Sturges, the vessel from which the Jungle Beauty Goddesses come to life.

# Table of Contents

# Chapter One

# Pretty Blue Ball

Open your eyes wide and look up. Look up high above the trees, the tallest buildings, the mountains, the birds, and the airplanes. Look beyond the puffy white clouds that layer the sky in the troposphere, the lowest part of the Earth's atmosphere. Close your eyes half-way, as if you are squinting, and look up as far as you can see into the stratosphere, beyond Ruppell's Vulture, the world's highest-flying bird. Keep looking even further than the brightest moon on the darkest night.

Take a deep breath, close your eyes, and imagine yourself levitating. Feel the tremendous jet stream wind whipping around your body at the speed of 199 miles per hour. Hold on tight, and look past the supersonic jet planes and the weather balloons as you ascend into the mesosphere. The air is very thin, and your body is shivering. The temperature is -100 c degrees cold. Keep your eyes closed and look up past the blazing light trails of the burning meteoroids. Notice the beautiful noctilucent clouds made of frozen water and ice crystals.

Close your eyes extremely tight and open your inner eye. Look even further up. You are now entering the thermosphere. Even though the temperature is - 1,500 c degrees, you will not feel it, so relax. Observe the hauntingly beautiful shades of blue, green, pink, red, and yellow lights that form the Earth's auroras. Notice the international space station and how the space shuttles and satellites orbit the atmosphere. You are more than 400 miles above Earth. This is where television pictures and phones calls are relayed by communication satellites that orbit Earth.

Keep your eyes closed and look even higher. The gravitational pull of Earth no longer exists, and you are now floating into outer space. You are surrounded by hydrogen and helium. Keep looking up. It is blacker than a million midnights, but for the sparkling lights from billions of galaxies.

Look up, up, up, up, and even further up. As you continue to travel skyward into the infiniteosphere, a multimillion miles from Earth, you will see the planet Ventopia, where karmic transformations have been thought to occur. Two miles west of Ventopia's prime meridian, on the plateau north of its Great Sea, lays Quark Drive. There you would see a magnificent iridescent palace made of diamonds with millions of buildings of many shapes and sizes that spread further than the eyes can see. Some of the buildings are topped with onion domes trimmed in silver in pastel colors of lavender, pink, and blue. The onion dome at the main entrance is pastel green and three sizes bigger than the other buildings.

The shimmering pearl stairs wind gracefully up to a purple stone door made of amethyst. On each side of that door is a majestic waterfall with lavender colored water. The grass, trees, and shrubbery along the pathway are various shades of pink. Upon entering the front door, the first thing noticed on the walls is a plethora of family pictures of the resident's children, with names such as Tlaloc, Ishatar, Buddha,Shapsu, Alator, Heng-O, Pangu, Shangdi, Isis, Aphrodite, Apollo, Brahma, Shiva, Freya and Jesus just to name a few.

Fifteen billion years ago, Dematter and his wife, Nebula, began to discuss the possibility of having children and creating the universe. At that time, they decided to wait a billion years, enjoying each other's company, before having children.

The love between Dematter and Nebula is more vast than the infinite cosmos. It has no beginning and no ending. Outer space is filled with the fragrant, hot ether of the excess breath of Dematter and Nebula's kisses. The meshing of their beings is the force of all of creation that ensues every dawn and dusk.

Upon rising and before sleep, Nebula devours Dematter's masculine energy that tastes like black licorice and ravishes his all-ness into a swooning pool of decadent gratification. The heat of his warm breath smells like cardamom as he suckles her neck and the peaks of her mountains that cause her inner being to be tormented in pleasure by the force of his burning desire.

Dematter merges with the essence of Nebula's velvety chocolate deliciousness. He feasts on her intoxicating beauty and absorbs the sweetness of her tender love. Dematter's tongue tantalizes every atom of Nebula's sumptuous curves, galaxies, and planets until she explodes blissfully throughout the boundless universe. Her feminine energy envelopes his throbbing virility into submission, and he succumbs into the divinity of her grace.

Approximately fourteen billion years ago, once they were ready to conceive, Dematter and Nebula kept their promise to each other and made love more passionately than they had ever done before. The volatile electric sparks from Dematter's and Nebula's kiss caused a Big Bang that birthed the universe. Dematter and Nebula agreed to give each birth-set of their children a beautiful planet ball as a present for their seven millionth birthdays. Their youngest set of children are about to reach that birthday. And so the story begins.

~~~

Nebula turns over to Dematter and whispers, "Honey, it's time." Dematter responds in a low, deep rumble, "I Know." As Nebula
~~~

massages her husband's shoulders, she says, "It's the seven millionth birthday of the septuplets. I think they are finally mature enough to take on the responsibility of developing and nurturing their own planet." Dematter's voice drops to a much softer and lower tone, as he sighs, "Nebula, these are my babies. I have had millions of other children, but Sahara, Kalahari, Qattara, Namib, Sinai, Chalbi, and Afar have always been daddy's little girls. They mean the universe to me. Dematter pauses. "I worry that after the initial excitement wears off, they may lose interest in their planetary duties."

Nebula nods her head as she smiles and says, "Honey, you are absolutely right; the girls are involved in so many other activities. Kalahari volunteers at the interstellar nursery; Qattara and Chalbi spend most of their time star-skiing, and the other girls are on the inter-galactic multicultural diversity committee. They are hardly ever home."

"Maybe we should postpone giving them their planet a few million years to give them more time to settle into the essence of being just goddesses. There is yet, still so much for them to learn about the vastness of the universe," Dematter reasons.

"Dem, stop worrying so much", Nebula says, "We have done our best to provide them with a supreme upbringing. They are beautiful, intelligent, conscientious, young godettes. They are looking forward to their initiation into deity-hood to become creators. They have told all of their friends and selected their ceremonial attire for the deity ball celebration. We can't disappoint them. Besides, honey, nothing could possibly go wrong. We are creators. It's who we are and what we do. Stop worrying so much."

~~~
~~~

**Kalahari's Voice**

*I am so excited because tomorrow, my sisters and I are going with our dad to select our planet to decorate with a plethora of life forms and guide their development. We are probably going to have a hard time selecting a planet that the seven of us will agree upon that would satisfy each one of our personalities. But the joy of traveling through space with my dad and sisters is such a pleasurable event that I don't really care if we ever find a planet.*

*I love my life here in Ventopia with my mother, my father, and my six sisters. I have never seen anyone capable of loving each other more deeply and intensely than the way which my parents love each other. My other siblings have created beings for their planets who profess their love for one another, but shortly thereafter, they break up or engage in acts of infidelity that destroy their beings' faith in love.*

*If my sisters and I ever find a planet, I want to create beings who know nothing but love. Un-evolved, negative emotions of hate, rage, and anger are simply the sloppy work of my sister Erida who wanted armies to fight each other for the sick pleasure of my brother Ares. Why bother to create a being just to watch them deliberately destroy themselves. Erida and Ares are pathetic, and I pity their beings that live on planet War. Daddy and mother did not raise us to rule our planets like this. How is it possible for beings to be born of nothing but love, yet learn how to hate themselves and others?*

*Many of my siblings have created life forms for their planets that they have grown to detest over time. I can't ever imagine hating a life form that I have created. It would feel like hating myself-- because, in essence it would be a part of me. In my opinion, the behavior of planetary beings is but a mere reflection of the gods and goddesses who created them. My sisters and I will create our beings with an abundance of overflowing love, and this is what our beings will give back in return.*

*I love my parents, and there is nothing that they could ever do or say that would stop me from loving them completely. When my sisters and I find a planet and create life forms for it, I know that our beings will love, honor, and respect us in the same manner that we love our parents. There is absolutely nothing that our beings could ever do to make me fear, envy, or despise them—because the ultimate purpose of being a deity is to forgive the unforgivable.*

~~~

The next morning, Dematter gazes proudly across the universe before focusing in on his seven daughters playfully throwing stardust at each other. He feels troubled because he knows that once his daughters take on the responsibility of caring for a planet, they will have very little time left to enjoy the freedom of being goddettes. So many of Dematter's children were anxious to become gods and goddesses before they were mature enough to rule a planet. They didn't understand that it was a privilege to be a spiritual being without an obligation to a planet and its
~~~

life forms. Goddettes are free to enjoy the wonderment of the exosphere without having to answer the prayers of their creations or worry about their evolvement.

Creating and caring for beings and planets is a tremendous responsibility that is not to be taken lightly. Even the most studious gods and goddesses make mistakes or miscalculate the proper chemical formula to sustain a planet with a life force. Dematter releases a breath of solar wind that causes the universe to shiver when he thinks about what they did to his son, Jesus, in the Cigar Galaxy on the planet Lleh. He begged him to wait before developing his planet with unrestricted thinking species, but he insisted on creating beings with free-will. His son believed that it was impossible to create and love a being that could fathom the thought of betraying its creator. But his son was wrong.

Dematter still remembers the day that they tied his son to a cross and attempted to kill him. What bothered Dematter the most is that the free-will thinking beings blamed his son's death on Natas. Even with their ability to think freely, they chose not to be accountable for his son's death. His son has completely forgiven them and still works tirelessly to let them know that he is their lord and savior.

Dematter knows that to keep the universe expanding and growing that he must relinquish some of his divine powers to his children—no matter how much it hurts. He ponders whether or not the girls are ready to handle the planetary Chi dust formula to bring their creations to life.

Dematter peers across the universe and smiles while watching his girls play. His curly long, black mustache and extensive, black, wavy, beard hang down his chest. Underneath his lips are barely visible as he mutters to himself, "My babies have never looked more innocent and sweet than they do at this very moment. I love them so much. Perhaps my wife is right; I am just being selfish." All of his other children have their own planets and have moved away from home.

Dematter puts on a stern face that is partially covered by his black hood covered in fur and calls his girls each by name to accompany him on the intergalactic journey to select their planet. "Kalahari, Sahara, Namib, Qattara, Chalbi, Sinai, and Afar—Come now!" Dematter shouts, "It's time to select your planet." As the girls star-skied over to their father, all seven of them screamed, "Daddy, daddy, we love you; you are the best daddy in the universe!" Dematter laughed hardily while saying, "I am the only father in the Universe. Flattery will get you everywhere."

Each girl takes a seat on the train of Dematter's long, over-flowing, blacker than a million-midnights, velvety, cape robe made of a mixture of dark energy and dark matter, covered sparsely by twinkling light shaped stars. The girls had always enjoyed inter-galactic travel with their father from the moment they were born; however, this was a special trip with their father they had been looking forward to.

As they traveled the universe, the girls reminisced and chatted with each other about how happy they were when their older siblings came home after selecting their planets; and discussed what characteristics they wanted for the beings they would create for their own planet.

"Remember when Zeus selected Namuh with the swirling vertical cloud stripes? Said Chalbi, "I love how it was surrounded by dozens of moons. I want something like that."

"Even though he is our brother, and I love him very much– I simply don't like the way he interacts with his beings, faux gods, and sexual tryst animals," Namib stated while frowning and rolling her eyes.

In a high pitched voice, with her hands on her hip, while moving her head from left to right, Kalahari said, "When daddy gives us our planet, it is our divine right to develop it as we please. I don't think it's nice to speak ill of our brother behind his back. I love Zeus."

"Kalahari, your naiveté is sickening, Sahara said, as she closed her eyes and placed hands on her beautiful bald head encircled with diamonds, "Do you really think that it is okay to use thunder and lightning as weapons to hurt less powerful beings--?"

"Ooooh, look!" shouted Afar as she stood up and pointed to their brother, Anansi's, beautiful spider galaxy. We should visit him soon; I miss his trickster stories."

"I love Gliese, Lakshmi's planet. It is the most beautiful pink ball that I have ever seen. She decorated it with lotus plants; her beings are beautiful, prosperous, wealthy women who ride on gigantic gray phantele, with long snouts and ears that look like the colocasia plants. The only sustenance that they need to survive on her planet is the plentiful milk that falls from ski and fills the oceans. I bet her creations love her so much." Kalahari says while folding her arms around her heart and hugging herself in an animated gesture of sheer delight.

Chalbi was staring off into the beautiful black universe. Everyone assumed that she was oblivious to the conversation when she nonchalantly said, "That sounds so boring. Who wants to live in la, la, land? Nothing ever changes. No one ever leaves the planet. They always look the exact same. A state of continual bliss is the exact same thing as being nonexistent. Those prosperous, beautiful women have no idea of how lucky they are because they have no other reference point."

Sahara says with a mocking laugh, as she raises her eyebrow, "Love her?—the last time I talked to Lakshmi, she told me that she felt a little sad because her beings never think about her because they always have everything that they need. I told her that she should take some things away from them so that they would stop taking her for granted. And then write some type of document with rules and rituals on how to live life. This special rule book will teach them how to communicate with her. However, she refuses to do it because it is the only way of life her beings know. Lakshmi said that she would have to destroy her beings and start over from the very beginning."

They all shake their heads together and shouted, "And daddy would never allow that to happen!"

Qattara takes a deep breath, leans back with her hands folded behind her head and gently nestles her head and body into the folds of her father's robe, and states, "I agree with you Chalbi, when we select our planet, let's make sure that our creations experience an evolution of being-ness. I don't want them to be like us. We will always look the same. Which is kind of neat—I guess. I mean, we really can't experience any other way of being; no matter how many billions of years pass, I can always recognize you. I will always know you exactly as you are. I want to experience a different type of reality vicariously through our creations."

"But in a sense, won't the essence of the beings that we create always be the same—because they will always be a part of us and we are the same," Namib says while gently running her fingers through her black, thick curly Mohawk.

"I haven't really thought about it much. But I think that everything evolves and grows in different ways," Sahara says. She stops talking to her sisters immediately and points to the Neuron Galaxy that they are flying past. "Daddy, I like the Niarb planet in the Neuron galaxy. My sisters and I could create beings who communicate telepathically. They could share lofty ideas about existence, help beings on other planets without hurting them because they wouldn't have a need for a body--"

"No way, Sahara!" Qattara interrupts, "that sounds so mind-numbing. No vessels for the beings to connect with others? This doesn't sound like fun to me."

Kalahari opens her eyes and mouth wide, places her crossed hands on her heart, and says, "Will they be able to love each other the way daddy loves us?"

"Better yet," Namib ponders out loud, "Will they have free-will after we create them, or will we have to babysit them so that they don't hurt themselves?"

Sinai asks, "What will they do to entertain themselves once we create them? Will they be able to experience joy and happiness, or will they simply live to die?

"Wait a minute, wait a minute," Afar says as she flirtatiously bounces her long, straight, brunette hair from side to side, "Will our beings be able to re-create themselves after we make the original beings? Do we want to take on this role as their creators or will they be responsible for keeping our planet populated?"

"Afar, you are right; we need to really think about this. Will our planet become overpopulated? How will we destroy things that are not working? How will we bring about change when something needs to evolve in a better way?" Chalbi asks.

"I hadn't thought about all of these things." Sahara apologizes, "Since we all must share in the responsibility of caring for our planet. Perhaps we should keep looking."

Dematter with his seven daughters sitting on the train of his long-black robe glide through the glimmering pitch-black universe sprinkled with an array of baby blue, white, pink, red, and yellow stars. The girls would sigh with delight each time they passed brilliant, colorful, billowy, swirls of misty hazes shaped like butterflies, horseheads, eagles, tarantulas, crabs, and some even appeared to look back at them with cat eyes. Even though they had taken this trip a million times with their parents, the soul-stirring beauty of their father's universe was his masterpiece that demanded nothing less than complete awe and submission to its beauty.

Hypnotized by the flamboyant lights of the elliptical, spiral, and irregular galaxies, the girls stopped talking and listened to the hum of the universe. Intergalactic travel was always exciting. Dematter and his seven daughters visited billions of galaxies, with each galaxy containing billions of planets in search of the perfect planet for his beloved daughters' seven millionth birthdays. They traveled through time that felt like an eternity. The search seemed hopeless. The girls could never find one planet that they all could agree upon. Although they are sisters born at the exact same time, on the same day, they had very distinct personalities.

Afar was always the most adventurous one, after they had ascended to the horizontal edges of infinity, she would jump off of her father's robe and hold on to the tail end of his robe's long train with both hands. Afar's creamy peach skin and baby blue eyes shimmered against the pitch-black universe. When she was a baby they tried to stop her from dangling off the edges of the train of Dematter's robe, and befriending the beings in the Andromeda Galaxy but realized that Afar has always been a free spirit and decided to trust her judgment. Afar lifted herself back onto her father's robe and snuggled up next to her sister Qattara. Qattara kissed Afar on her cheek, braided her long brown hair and twisted it into a bun, and softly whispered, "I love you sister. One as the same, the same as one--without you- there would be none."

Qattara took off her long, redhead wrap and placed it over her sister Afar and herself and yawned, "Daddy, could you please take us home. I don't think we will ever find the perfect planet that my sisters and I will all agree upon."

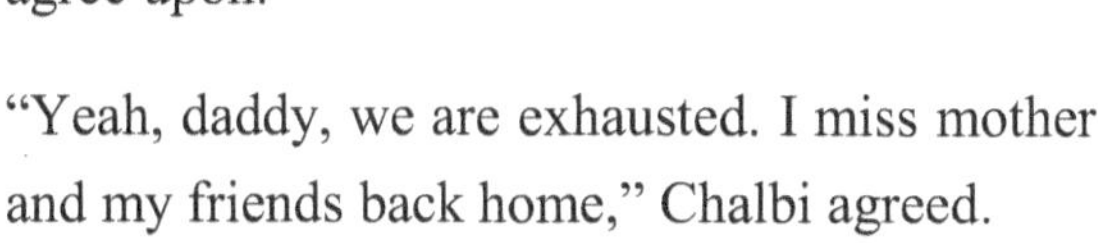

"Yeah, daddy, we are exhausted. I miss mother and my friends back home," Chalbi agreed.

Kalahari sighed, "Daddy, all that really matters is that we know that you love us; maybe we are not meant to take care of our own planet."

Exhausted, disappointed, and sad, the girls were convinced that they would never find a planet that they all could agree upon for their seven millionth birthday.

"Well, girls, I have one more galaxy to show you before we return home. It's called the Milky Way Galaxy, and it's one of my favorite places in the universe. It's my secret hideaway; it's where I go to originate new ideas and relax with your mother."

"Daddy, I doubt if we will find a planet that all seven of us can agree on. We are all so different. Daddy, can we just, please, please go home?" Sinai begged. As Dematter enters the Orion arm of the Milky Way Galaxy, all seven of the girls scream together, "Daddy, Daddy, Daddy, we want the pretty blue ball— please Daddy give us the pretty blue ball!"

## Chapter Two

# The Deity Ball

Deity Balls have always been a special event for Dematter and his wife, Nebula. This is the only occasion where it is mandatory for the entire family and highest divinity members of the universe to come together to celebrate the transition from being a godette to becoming gods and goddesses with planetary duties and responsibilities. The day before the big event, Nebula and her sister Celestia busied themselves designing ceremonial deity ball gowns that match the color of the Pretty Blue Ball planet that the sisters selected to cultivate. Each ball gown was made of a luxurious, vibrant royal blue taffeta with a fitted, cut-off the shoulder bodice with a décolleté neckline trimmed in white lace and dangling green pearls. The bottom half of the ballroom gown was an enormous double-layered bubble full skirt enhanced with green and golden bronze flower rosettes.

Nebula enjoyed nothing more than decorating her iridescent palace that she designed from top to bottom. She hung intricate, elegant purple diamond chandeliers of various sizes from the high ceiling in the main ballroom. Celestia sent violet dwarf star invitations that lit up the beautiful black universe to their entire family, all of the archangels, angels, divine beings, and spiritual guides and teachers from the Karmic Transformation planet.

Meanwhile, Dematter had two important tasks that he had to tend to before the Deity Ball. His first task was to set up the girl's planetary development station located a quinquagintacentacentillion miles up from the Pretty Blue Ball planet into the exosphere. This is where Dematter's children, who are gods and goddesses are required to consistently monitor their planets and construct the DNA coding for the physical appearance and behavior of their beings of all sizes and shapes. They are also required to encode a dogma of karmic rules and laws of attraction for them as well. It is customary for the gods and goddesses to monitor, protect, and provide assistance to their beings. Some gods and goddesses have actually visited their planets but, Dematter is adamantly against this because of the imbalance of chi energy that always has a negative effect on the beings created by the gods and goddesses.

While setting up the planetary development station for his daughter's planet, Dematter stayed for a while to chat and share a few laughs with Apollo, Shiva, and Buddha. He asked Athena and Neith about how their planets were progressing, and they told him that everything was going great. Both sisters expressed to their father that they were looking forward to attending the Deity Ball to witness their youngest sisters' take their vows to become goddesses.

Dematter's second important task prior to the Deity Ball was to go back to the Milky Way Galaxy and remove the Pretty Blue Ball planet Earth from its orbit and put in its place a temporary faux planet to maintain the balance of the solar system. He then took the Pretty Blue Ball planet Earth back to his workshop in the infinite-sphere to give it some final changes before presenting it to the girls at the Deity Ball.

Dematter placed a magnetic device in the core of the Pretty Blue Ball planet to correspond to its planetary development center station so that the energy of the Earth and its beings would be in sync with his daughter's instructions. But most importantly, he named some of Earth's future deserts after his daughters.

**Sinai's Voice**

*After my sisters and I selected our planet Earth, we split up and leisurely explored the surrounding outer space to gather data for future ideas on how we planned to go about developing our planet Earth after the Deity Ball Ceremony. I noticed a magnetic, beautiful, celestial body that was reflecting light from the sun that lit up Earth's night sky. I decided to visit and landed on the side, facing away from the Earth.*

*When I arrived, I saw the most striking man that I have ever seen in my life smoking a pipe, drinking nectar, and reading. His body was gray all over, and his head was shaped like a crescent moon. He looked up from his reading materials, and we stared deeply into each other's eyes for what felt like an eternity. We fell madly in love at that very moment, but neither of us knew it at the time.*

*I apologized for interrupting him, and he beckoned me to stay. He put down his pipe, asked me my name, and offered me a drink. I told him that my name was unimportant in fear that he would know more about me than I was willing to reveal. Given that my father, Dematter, is creator of the universe my reputation precedes me, and this would destroy my chances of ever finding someone to love me just for me.*

*He introduced himself to me as Dr. Lunar M. Crater. I told him that his planet was desolate and that he looked so lonely and sad. I asked him if his planet had suffered from some unspeakable misfortune that had annihilated all of its beings. He said that he was never lucky enough to lose a loved one because he has always been the only being on the moon. He explained to me that he did not live on a planet but a natural satellite of a planet. He went on to clarify that because he is not a planet he was not created by or owned by gods and goddesses.*

*He poured me a glass of nectar, and we talked about everything and nothing at all. After a few drinks, I told him that I needed to leave and suggested that maybe our paths would cross again. He asked me how could he contact me in the future, and I told him that it would be impossible. He kissed me on the cheek and revealed to me that he felt a connection with me that he had never felt for another being. He then kissed my lips and said, "When you leave you are taking my heart with you because I am incapable of ever loving another being."*

*I asked him, "How can you proclaim to love me when you don't even know my name?" He said, "I don't need to know your name to love you. Your name is but a label that traps and wraps you into the expectations of others. Knowing your name will have no bearing on the depth of what I feel for you at this very moment in time-- no matter what your name is or isn't, it doesn't change the essence of your being."*

*He began to kiss me on my neck slowly, and I muttered to him, "but we have just met…" "I am who I am, and you are who you are," Mr. Crater said, "No matter how much time passes, we both will always remain the same. In fact our love is more likely to wane in time. Our desire for each other will never be as pure as it is this very moment. Time taints, fades, and erodes everything. The magic of the moment is the only force that intensifies existence." I passionately kissed him, and we merged as one.*

*What Mr. Crater did not know is that after the Deity Ball in the near future that I would no longer be the same free spirit. I am now a godette without planetary duties and responsibilities, so in a sense I am free to do whatever I want before I take my vows to nurture and develop planet Earth. I decided until the Deity Ball I would engage in a love affair with Lunar until I am officially ordained as a goddess so as not to disobey the laws of deity-hood or destroy my family's reputation.*

*I told him that since he did not know my name, I would feel more comfortable if he would allow me to call him Mr. Moon Man Lover. He loved me with every particle of his soul, but what he did not know is that I can only love him on my terms—if at all. The beauty of the moment is that it has no expectations, hopes, or rules.*

~~~

The night before the ball, the seven sisters could not sleep because they were anticipating what it would be like to develop a planet and create new beings. They joked about how their brother Jesus always insisted upon bringing the wine; and how their sister Aphrodite would bring no less than five boyfriends who were all madly in love with her. In the midst of all the laughing and talking, Sinai's laughter turned into a soft sniffle as tears rolled down her dark brown face.

"What's wrong," Qattara asked while hugging Sinai and removing her long black curly hair from her face.

"I like things the way they are now. I like being in the moment. I like star-skiing and riding on the train of daddy's robe across the universe. I am not looking forward to worrying about how to make another being happy. I am already happy."
~~~

"Well, I'm not happy at all. I am bored," Chalbi said with her face buried down in her pillow. "I can't wait to blow up some stuff. Watching stars explode is getting kind of old. I want in on some real action."

"Maybe we can ask daddy if we can put it off for another million years," Kalahari says while sitting on her bed with her legs crossed and arms folded behind her head. "At the interstellar nursery we are creating these awesome new stars for a new galaxy—"

"Please enough! Just go to sleep," Namib yells with her silk blanket covering her short bushy Mohawk. "Tomorrow is a long day. We are going to take our vows. Please. Let's just refresh our spirits and be ready in the morning to accept our new responsibilities."

The next morning the sisters drank lavender tea and ate their mom's magnificent manna muffins before preparing to dress for the ball. Nebula and Celestia helped them put on their matching royal blue ceremonial, astral gowns for the Deity Ball. An awkward silence filled the room. It was hard to believe that Kalahari and Afar were not chattering away about the intergalactic cultural diversity committee or the latest gossip about their sibling's planets.

After the girls were dressed for the ball, they walked with their mother, Nebula, to a faraway courtyard; where they sat peacefully on iridescent white opal benches; under thick, tall trees with heart-shaped pink leaves that gathered around a small lavender lake with a large rainbow-colored fountain in the center with several ascending layers of water-- each layer higher than the next.

**Kalahari's** toasted tan face looked especially beautiful. Her golden crinkled shoulder-length hair fell softly on her shoulders; sparkling emerald green eyes, and butterfly-shaped mauve-pink lips complimented the green flowers on her royal blue ball gown. Kalahari sat next to **Sahara,** whose elegant shiny band of diamonds surrounding her perfectly shaped bald head paled in comparison to her dark brown purplish skin, reddish-pink voluptuous lips, and piercing royal blue eyes. Sahara was as beautiful as a black starry night. Sahara held Qattara's hand.

**Qattara's** broad facial features looked gorgeous under her burnt sienna skin, brown and bronze eyes, and bright red full lips. She looked regal in her head wrap that matched her ball gown. Qattara rested her hand on Namib's lap, who sat next to her.

Royal blue and green jewels decorated each side of **Namib's** Mohawk. Like her mother, Nebula, Namib's large round eyes were lavender and violet. Her purple lips dominated her face, and even when she is happy, she always looked sad. Even while wearing her ultra-feminine, astral ball gown, Namib still looked like an amazon warrior. Her foot playfully touched Sinai's foot who sat next to her.

**Sinai** looked like black royalty of the night in her ball gown. Her sea-green eyes and hot pink lips glowed against her dark brown skin and long black curly hair. Sinai placed her arm around **Chalbi's** waist who was sitting next to her with her protruding, shocking orange lips, metallic brown eyes, and long wavy black hair that looked dangerously beautiful flattering her dark bronze skin. Anyone could see that she wore the ball gown because she had no other choice; still the green flowers and white silk trim could not soften the fierce look in her eyes as she placed her arms around Afar who was sitting next to her.

**Afar's** delicate facial features, dazzling bright baby blue eyes, and red lips highlighted her creamy peach smooth skin. Her long wavy brunette hair covered her ball gown over each breast. She looked like a princess of the stars as she laid her head on Kalahari's shoulder, who sat next to her.

The seven sisters waited quietly and patiently until it was time for their mother to escort them back to the ballroom alter to take their vows. Nebula kissed each one of her daughters on the cheek before leaving the courtyard. When she was far away out of their sight, Nebula knelt down under a luscious lavender tree, with long willowy hanging branches. The plush tall, pink grass was speckled with bright yellow flowers shaped like butterflies that enveloped her entire body as she sobbed.

One foot away from the tree was a babbling brook where sparkling clear lavender water trickled over various shapes and sizes of rock-sized turquoise gemstones. The beautiful snake dragons relaxed in the trees and chased each other along the banks of the babbling brook. The winged snake dragons have long slender bodies, big lips, forked tongues, pointy ears, and mermaid tails. They come in every color and pattern imaginable, and they are originally from Ventopia.

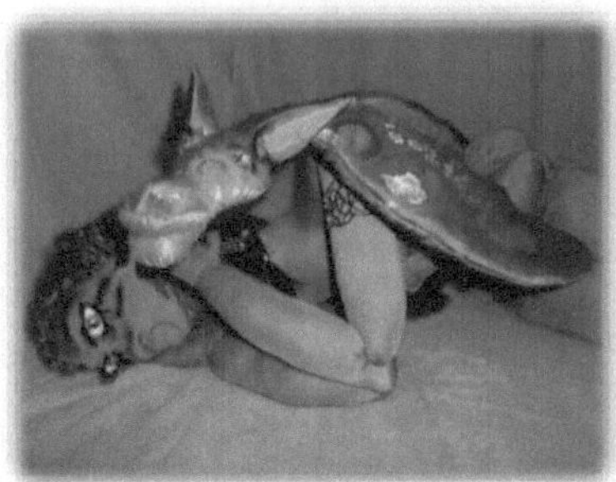

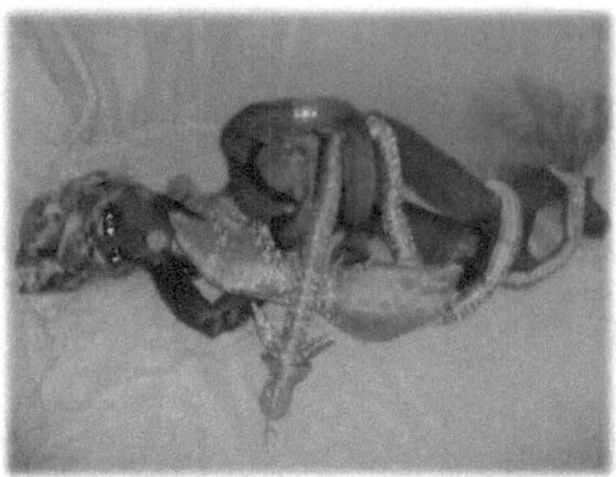

Unlike Dematter and Nebula's other children, the septuplets loved to play with the snake dragons from the moment that they were conceived. They each selected a snake dragon and gave them a special name. In fact, the bond between them and their pet snake dragons are so close that they created a special language and learned how to communicate telepathically with them. The girls used the snake dragons to send messages to each other when they were galaxies apart. Seeing the snake dragons made Nebula especially sad because they reminded her of the playful spirit of her girls that would be forever usurped by their planetary duties.

This is Nebula's favorite place in the universe. This is the garden that keeps her deepest and darkest secrets. She never cries in front of her husband. Nebula never cries in front of anyone. She feels that it is her spiritual duty to be Dematter's emotional rock that he can always depend on. Before Dematter created the universe, he was spontaneous, fun, happy, and free-spirited. He lavished her in his love. Now that they have children, Dematter never stops worrying about their children's well-being, and his heart is always heavy and filled with anxiety.

She feels that because she is the one who really wanted to have children-- and not him— it is her fault that her husband must bear the burden of being the all-knowing, omniscience creator of the universe who refuses to meddle with his children's life choices. Dematter had always been a loving and giving man, and Nebula felt responsible for taking his love and using it against him. He created the universe to give their children a home life rich with meaning. But since having the children, Dematter had become a reserved and cautious man. He made a decision before their children were born that he would never blur their paths of free-will and destiny. And he would only agree to have children if Nebula promised to never interfere with the journey that each child must take to reach his or her full potential--no matter how painful the consequences are. Nebula wholeheartedly agreed with her husband because she knows that they are immortal beings. And since losing a child forever was not a feasible option; she felt that she could handle any other challenges of being a parent.

Nebula would never admit to Dematter that she, too, was worried sick that the septuplets were not ready to create beings and develop a planet. Nebula tried to ignore the unsettling energy that twitched in the pit of her being; but like any mother, she knows her children well, and she knew that the septuplets were not ready for the responsibility of being goddesses.

Nebula noticed that Namib was hesitant about creating new beings without giving them a clearly defined purpose. She told her mother numerous times that she had no desire to babysit un-evolved beings.

Nebula feared that Kalahari's obsession with wanting to help beings love each other and to love her as their goddess would cause her to make terrible decisions that could backfire and cause unintentional destruction. Sahara believes that every emotion, decision, and behavior can be rationally and logically manipulated and analyzed to get whatever results she wants from her beings. Nebula was convinced that Sahara's way of thinking would create detrimental conditions for the beings on her planet.

'Qattara is my compassionate baby,' Nebula thought to herself. 'She will do a great job with beings in a high-density atmosphere because she seems to understand the importance of tangible consequences and rewards. I know that her biggest weakness will be siding with her sisters even when she knows that they are wrong.'

Nebula worried about Chalbi because she is the most excited about ruling a planet than the other sisters. She would spend summers with her brother Zeus who taught her several veracious ways to destroy lesser beings. Chalbi's favorite saying is, "There is no point in having power if you don't plan to use it."

Nebula knows that Sinai is depressed about becoming a goddess because she doesn't like to think about the past or the future. She is the most spontaneous of the septuplets. Sinai is the most like her father prior to him creating the universe. Sinai's spirit believes in the magic of the moment, but nurturing new beings and a planet will force her to discipline herself to commit to rules and planning.

Afar has never understood the significance of boundaries. She is the most creative of all the sisters. If something doesn't exist, she believes that it should be created. The problem is that she never thinks about the long-term consequences of combining energies and forces from different worlds, with opposing agendas, and unbalanced relationships.

"They are not ready," Nebula cried with her hands covering her face, almost touching the ground as if she was telling it a secret. "Why did I beg my husband to have children? I thought that they would be extensions of ourselves that we could perfect, love, and control. I never realized that just because you create something, it doesn't mean that it belongs to you."

Nebula knew that the babbling brook was not babbling at all. It was clearly telling her that as always, her children will be fine and not to worry. She took a deep breath, stood up and brushed the wrinkles from her violet, velvet dress with amethyst and opal gemstones around the neckline, the hemline of its long train, and the circumference of its long wide sleeves.

Nebula's long wavy black hair hung mid-way down her back, each side, and the middle of her hair had purple streaks that highlighted her purple and black eyelashes. Her lavender and purple eyes complimented her dark brown face and full purple lips. Dematter loved the round voluptuous shape of Nebula's breasts and buttocks so much that he created the circular planets in the universe in honor of her beauty. Her husband considered her to be the most beautiful woman in the universe beyond compare.

Nebula walked back to the palace's ballroom to see if her husband, Dematter, was ready to begin the ceremony. When she arrived she was greeted by several of her children with kisses and hugs. The archway and path to the altar was lit by angels wearing flowing white gowns trimmed in gold, holding white candles. Archangels were standing on both sides of the altar. The room smelled like sandalwood, frankincense, and myrrh. The lavender diamond chandeliers with dangling pearls sparkled. The guests were softly humming aum that caused the angel's feathers to slightly sway to the rhythm of the humming sound.

Nebula walks into a private room in the back of the ballroom where she finds her husband looking sadder than she had ever seen him before. She cradles his head into the cleavage of her buxom breasts and kisses him on top of his black, glistening, bald head several times.

She feels his warm breath against her aching heart as he sighs, "No more, Love of my Life." She continues to softly kiss his head all the way to his ear and then whispers into his ear, "I know," Nebula says while hugging him, "As we agreed, this is the last time—no more children."

He lifted his head from her cleavage and began to kiss her forehead, the lid of each eye, and then each cheek before passionately kissing her lips. He then used his tongue to sway tenderly her words of doubt into submission. Dematter gazed deep into Nebula's eyes and said, "It's time."

"I'll go get the girls," she murmured before leaving the room as she ran her fingers through her hair and straightened her dress to regain her poise from being enraptured into the throws of desire of her husband's love.

When Nebula arrived back to the courtyard to escort her daughters back to the ballroom, each godette gracefully stood up one after the other, until all seven were standing. They looked at their mother expectantly. Nebula slowly nodded her head, turned around and headed back to the Deity Ball with her seven daughters following behind her in their flowing royal blue ball gowns. They walked in silence.

Nebula and her daughters entered the ballroom and began walking down the center aisle as angels played their violins and harps, and the honored guests in attendance hummed along in unison. At the base of the altar, flanked by two archangels, stood their father, Dematter, the long train of his black robe draped upon the rose quartz floor. The seven sisters looked straight ahead as if they were hypnotized by the sight of their father holding both arms straight up with his fingers wide apart as his palms cradled the enormous, breathtakingly beautiful royal blue ball with white misty clouds of swirls, and patches of green with bronze and yellow trimmings.

The Pretty Blue Ball planet appeared to move in and out as if it were breathing, as Dematter held it over his head. The hauntingly beautiful royal blue glow from the planet became the only light that lit the entire room. As the music continued to play, Nebula walked up the aisle to stand next to her husband as the seven sisters waltzed to position themselves in a crescent shape around their parents standing at the altar. Namib, Sahara, Qattara, Kalahari, Sinai, Chalbi and Afar bowed down on both knees and stretched their arms out in front of them, with their palms of their hands flat on the rose quartz floor. In sync, the seven sisters lowered their heads waiting to take their vows from their father.

Dematter said while holding the Earth over his head in a loud, voluminous, deep, tone; "Namib, Sahara, Kalahari, Qattara, Sinai, Chalbi, and Afar, do you promise to forsake all others and dedicate and commit your lives to developing, nurturing, and protecting the Pretty Blue Ball planet Earth and all of its being big and small until the death of its sun?"

All seven of the sisters say together, "Yes, father, we will."

Do you promise to love and cherish your beings and cultivate this planet Earth in a manner that will nourish their bodies, develop their minds, inspire their spirits, and evolve their souls for a life of eternal reincarnation with compassion, integrity, and wisdom?

All seven of the sisters say together, "Yes, father, we shall."

Do you promise never to use your life –giving chi powers to harm, abuse, destroy, or intercede in the affairs of your beings and the natural cause and effect laws that exist between them and their home-- planet Earth?

All seven of the sisters say together, "Yes, father, we do."

Do you promise to never, ever under any circumstances violate or exploit the spiritual, physical, and psychological growth of your beings by intermingling, socializing, or befriending them in a way that will prevent them from reaching their full potential in a manner that is self-selective, self-reflective and none-destructive?

All seven of the sisters say together, "Yes, father, we do."

The Sanskrit meaning of the word jungle means uncultivated land, but now you are the ordained cultivators of the Pretty Blue Ball planet Earth. Jungle is now the collective first name each of you will carry in matrimony to the Pretty Blue Ball planet Earth.

As creators, you must entrench this planet and all of its beings with a soul-stirring, healing beauty that reflects the careful, meticulous, splendorous design of the universe from which you were born. May I have your word?

All seven of the sisters say together, "Yes, father, we shall."

From this moment forward, Beauty is now your collective second name to remind you that beauty is a detailed act of craftsmanship that reflects the soul of its creator.

One-third of planet Earth is made up of deserts with extreme arid, cold, and hot conditions that resemble the intergalactic atmosphere of home. It was predestined that each one of you have been named after a desert as reminders to you of the all-encompassing love of your mother and I—each grain of sand is symbolic of how much we love and will miss each one of you-- and that you are never far away from home.

Dematter reaches forward with planet Earth in his hand, and the seven sisters stand up and collectively reach out to place both hands on the Pretty Blue Ball planet with their father to take their final vows.

As the creator of the universe and all that there is, all that there ever was, and all that there ever will be-- with the everlasting love and support of my wife Nebula, we now imbue you with creative powers to cultivate the Pretty Blue Ball planet Earth and all of its being until its sun releases its energy force back into the universe. Do you promise to serve this planet and all of its beings with kindness, honor, compassion, and integrity?

All seven of the sisters said together, "Yes, father, we do."

"By the power invested in me, you are no longer godettes. You have taken your vows, and you are now entrusted and are held accountable as creators and protectors of the Pretty Blue Ball planet Earth and all of its beings. From this moment forward, you shall be called Jungle Beauty Goddesses rulers of the Pretty Blue Ball planet Earth.

Dematter let go of the Pretty Blue Ball planet, and it was held up high by all seven of the Jungle Beauty Goddesses. Everyone cheered. It was a blissful event.

## Chapter Three

# The Perfect Creature

*I am so glad that that ridiculous Deity Ball is over; those big puffy gowns, those whining instruments, and those singing angels were more than I could bear. Since my parents promised not to have any more children, at least I don't have to worry about attending another torturous affair.*

*This is probably going to be the last night that my sisters and I stay here at home in the palace with our parents. This I will miss. I will miss riding through the galaxy on the long black train of daddy's robe with my sisters Qattara, Sinai, Afar, Sahara, Kalahari, and Namib. I will miss my mother's beautiful smile, lavender tea, and manna muffins each morning—but what I won't miss is the predictability of each day.*

*Every day was pretty much the same at home. Despite this, my favorite activity is still watching the stars explode. It is the most magnificent event in the universe.*

*When the stars explode, it releases a vibrant, colorful cloud of dust that releases chemicals such as iron, lithium, hydrogen, silicon, oxygen, carbon-- in fact every substance in the universe. These are the interstellar factories that my father created that makeup ninety-nine percent of the chi dust that he uses to create life. One percent of the chi dust is an element that only my father has access to.*

*Some of my siblings think that I am negative because I enjoy watching things dramatically change forms; but every death is a rebirth. Every ending is a beginning. Motion is a combination of order and disorder.*

*Tomorrow my sisters and I will go to the planetary development station to begin cultivating our Pretty Blue Ball planet and creating life forms. I know that we are going to disagree about what life forms we should create with our chi dust that daddy gave us after the Deity Ball, but I plan to put my foot down on this one. I put up with their prissiness long enough. Now it's my turn. I am so disgusted with this whole belief in creating a complex being. Haven't they seen the drama that our siblings had gone through when they created beings with feelings, issues, problems, emotions, and purposes? I don't have time to play goddess of lesser beings. It's overdone, boring, and trite.*

*I want to create humongous, magnificent creatures that don't ask questions and fend for themselves. I want to construct a creature where their mere existence says, "I am here dammit move out of my way." I want to utilize the entire voluminous space of the Earthball. I want the vastness of my creatures to cause the Earth to tremble each time it breathes. The challenge is that I must convince my sisters to agree to this.*

*I think what I am going to do is exploit each one of their weaknesses— no, I mean strengths-- and use it against them. Kalahari is such a cry baby. She really gets on my nerve with all of her talk about love, love, love. How sickening. The only love that she knows is the undying love of our parents, our sibling set, and maybe me on the days that I don't want to strangle her. I will tell Kalahari that love doesn't work all the time because it comes in various amounts. The life forms that have the least amount of love will always be the most powerful beings. They will prey on and destroy beings that are kind and loving.*

*I will tell Qattara that the beings that we create should live freely without worrying about the restraints of their physical bodies. Life forms should not have to worry about how they look to others or themselves. What difference does it make? They shouldn't have to worry about what they eat or who they eat. They should live and do as they please. This is my plan.*

*Sinai will be the easiest to get on my side; she believes in living in the now. No past, no history, or no future. Only the present moment is important. Here, here sister! It will be tough to get Namib on my side because she believes that the ultimate goal of any being is to become self-directed and self-reflective. The beings that I have in mind won't think at all—and after they die, their chi dust will dissipate into the stars without all of the karmic drama of complex beings.*

*Sahara is definitely an ally. She logically understands that it is in everyone's best interest to focus on a being that does not destroy the Earth but feeds on it for survival. Sahara will appreciate creating a life force that does not beg for things from us or who is helpless and can't defend itself. I don't want to create a being that has to praise and honor me for bringing it into existence. Hey, you are there, and I am here; you do your thing I will do mine. Live and let live.*

*Afar is a little naïve. She loves creating new things. It shouldn't be that hard to convince her to try out my idea to make the most monstrous creatures of all time. I think I will call them dinosaurs. Yes, beautiful big creatures who mind their own business.*

~~~

The next morning, Dematter took his seven daughters and their planet Earth to the planetary development station so that the girls could begin creating various life forms. He hugged and kissed each daughter before he left. And while flying away, he told them that he was proud of them and that he had faith in their ability to do a good job.

The Jungle Beauty Goddesses quickly mixed a portion of their chi dust and began beautifying their planet Earth with trees, grass, birds, and fish of different shapes, sizes, and colors. They got along magnificently as they sat around the beautiful blue planet while decorating it with various exotic life forms. First they would draw a picture and then encode the DNA instructions into the planetary work station that was hooked up to the Earth. They would predetermine each species mating habits, how many off-springs it would reproduce, what they should eat, who would be their primary predators, what type environmental conditions it would need to survive, how long it should live, and how it should look-- down to the smallest detail of how many hairs or feathers it should have, its colors, shapes, and pattern.

The Jungle Beauty Goddesses decided to create the first life forms for their beautiful planet that could live only in the seas. There are very few planets in the universe that have water, so they thought that it would be challenging to create life forms that could survive in this element. Before making bigger creatures, the sisters decided first to make very small animals have a better understanding of how their chi dust could work together to create various life forms. One of the very first intricate
~~~

life forms that they created together was trilobites who ranged in size from one to twelve inches. Tribolites had three body segments, a hard shell, jointed legs attached to a spine, and hard crystal eyes. The sisters were so excited because this life form was a big improvement from the worms they had originally created. They all agreed that it made more sense for the trilobites to eat the worms; than to spend their time and energy killing billions of worms that had already multiplied.

Once the sisters got the hang of DNA coding, they designed more creatures for the oceans and seas such as seashells, sea urchins, starfish, corals, sea urchins, scorpions, and Haikouichthys fish. After enough practice Chalbi produced a 17 feet cameraceras, shaped like a long, thin cone with several tentacles. It preyed on their other life forms, but its size and shape made it fascinating to watch.

The Jungle Beauty Goddesses enjoyed the variety of creatures that lived in the seas and oceans, but they thought it would be intriguing to create creatures that could live in the sea and on land. They thought that it would be best if the animals could live in both environments, in the unfortunate tragic event that they were unable to sustain proper oxygen levels to maintain life on land. Some of the first life forms that they created that could live in the seas and on the land included salamanders, frogs, and turtles. The sisters clapped their hands together over their heads and screamed to celebrate their success.

They created large tree-sized fern plants on land that pumped oxygen into the air. They noticed that Earth's landmass was hot, humid, and moist and that the trees that they had planted had multiplied and created a swampy atmosphere that produced an oxygen-rich environment. The sisters decided that it was time to focus most of their creative energy on producing life forms that could thrive primarily on land. This was the most fun that the sisters had had together in a long time. They made up songs and sang together. They imitated the faces of some of their creatures and made each other laugh uncontrollably. They performed silly dances while holding hands dancing around their Pretty Blue Ball planet.

They fashioned winged creatures such as butterflies with dainty patterns, red ladybugs with black spots, golden yellow bumblebees with black strips, and dragonflies with shimmery double wings. They made creatures without wings such as spiders, termites, roaches, and ants that crawled through every nook and cranny of the forest grounds. They agreed on what type of fruits, vegetables, and flowers to make. After crafting the flowers they would playfully place them in each other's hair.

The Earth was even more beautiful now. Everything knew where it belonged and was doing what it was designed to do. The Jungle Beauty Goddesses sighed with relief at how well they had all gotten along. Chalbi thought that this would be the perfect time to suggest that they create bigger life forms to utilize the plush vegetation that covered the Earth. The other sisters vehemently disagreed. They wanted to create complex beings with creative powers and self-awareness.

Chalbi told her sisters that she had an idea for creatures that would roam the Earth and give them the freedom to continue in their intergalactic activities. The other sisters couldn't imagine what type of life form that they could create that was similar to their nature and needed very little of their time and attention. Chalbi arranged a meeting with her sisters to reveal to them a detailed plan of why they should create dinosaurs. She even served lavender tea and had her mother send manna muffins that she served to her sisters.

While sipping the last of her lavender tea, Afar asked, "Chalbi, why are you being so nice to us? Is something wrong? Are you really our sister?" She nervously smiled while setting her teacup on the table.

After the sisters finished chatting and eating, Chalbi said, "We are having such an incredible time together that I almost forgot why I called this meeting. I have had so much fun developing our Pretty Blue ball with the best sisters in the universe. I have a great idea for life forms that will be able to utilize the overgrowth of the humongous trees, plants, forests, and moist swamp-like conditions on our planet. Chalbi sipped her lavender tea and took a deep breath before continuing. She waved her hands and created a hologram illustration with neon light blue lines of a dinosaur that stood in the middle of the table surrounded by the sisters. The six sisters gasped with disbelief.

*Chalbi said, "No, relax. Listen, dear sisters. The dinosaurs are the perfect creatures for planet Earth. Kalahari, Sinai, and Afar, I know how you feel about violence and preying on other species. So, I thought that I... I mean we... could encode their DNA to be herbivorous so that they don't eat each other. They will only eat the plush plants, vegetation, and tree branches. They won't bother the magnificent creatures that we made that live in the oceans and seas. We can make them in various sizes from seven to one hundred feet tall. They would be gigantic and could travel the span of the Earth. They would lay eggs and not have to worry about being the product of inadequate parenting or developing emotional attachments to other beings. And I thought that we could give them long, elegant, graceful necks like ours and long tails like our pet snake dragons back home.*

~~~

To Chalbi's surprise, Namib was the first sister to support her idea. Namib said that this was an awesome idea because they wouldn't have to spend time helping complex being discovered their life purposes and assist them with a plethora of "why me questions." Sinai and Sahara were intrigued by the idea and thought that it was worth giving a try. Qattara, Afar, and Kalahari were very disappointed because they were
~~~

looking forward to creating a more sophisticated type being with god-like qualities; but eventually decided to give the dinosaurs a trial period because their love for their sisters superseded their hatred for dinosaurs.

The sisters voted, and they all agreed that some dinosaurs would be herbivores, and the smaller ones would be carnivores. Chalbi was happy that she was able to convince her sisters to see the advantages of seeing things her way. She manipulated her sisters into creating cold-blooded dinosaurs who laid eggs that hatched with no emotional attachment to its creator. Chalbi was very contented and happy with this arrangement because it gave her more time to spend with her brother Apollo.

Namib created a dimetrodon and anedaphosaurus with beautiful sails on their backs, similar to her Mohawk. Chalbi created a ten feet long gorgonops with 14 inches long, sharp canine teeth that hung outside their lips. Sinai made a diictodon a cute little thing with tusks sticking out from the upper jaw that had five claws on each paw. Kalahari and Afar collaborated and surprised everyone by making a meganeura that looked like a dragonfly with a 2 feet wingspan. The Jungle Beauty

Goddesses began competing with each other to see who could create the biggest creatures. Chalbi made the giganotosaurus, and Qattara created the argentinosaurus. Sahara made the tyrannosaurus and the Torosaurus.

Chalbi created the therizinosaraus; it had a long neck, small head, with three feet claws on each hand. She wanted it to use its humongous claws to stab other dinosaurs and pick their eyes out of their sockets before killing them—but Kalahari, Qattara, and Afar refused to participate, so she agreed to make them herbivorous. The therizinosaraus used its enormously sharp, long claws to reach high in the trees to gather leaves and branches for dinner.

*"How boring, I compromised because I didn't want my sisters to stop contributing their chi dust to the development of the dinosaurs."Chalbi thought to herself.*

The sisters agreed that they needed a dinosaur for the sky, so together, they created the pteranodon with a vast wingspan of 30 feet. The sisters marveled at how magnificent they looked gliding from coast to coast. Of course it was Namib's idea to place a head crest on the males. She loved creating things that looked similar to her Mohawk. Sinai created a 10 feet tall phorusrhacus bird with small wings that could not fly. It could stalk its prey and run 40 miles an hour and kill it with its beak. Chalbi, Sahara, and Namib were thoroughly entertained by watching it terrorize other animals. They incessantly teased Sinai for creating a bird with wings that was unable to fly. They insisted that she encode the phorusrhacus bird DNA to be carnivorous so that it would have a better chance of survival on land. As a joke, the sisters decided to give many of the dinosaur's feathers because they thought it was ridiculously cute and funny; and it reminded them of their pet snake dragons from home.

The Pretty Blue Ball Planet was teeming with life; everything was perfect. Earth was filled with an abundance of beautiful big and small creatures that roamed the land, swam in the seas and oceans, and flew through the clouds. The sisters parted ways for millions of years to continue their intergalactic activities and left their Pretty Blue Ball planet unattended. They were not stressed out with the daily demands of monitoring their planet. With so much free time available to them, the Jungle Beauty Goddesses were able to visit their parents and siblings from other galaxies, star-ski, and participate in their intergalactic committee activities.

Kalahari, Afar, and Qattara were becoming increasingly unhappy with the dinosaurs. They complained about being bored and felt that they had not put any real effort or care into creating their life forms. They called a meeting for all of the sisters to come together to discuss a strategy on how to get rid of the dinosaurs to make room for more sophisticated beings who reflected some characteristics of their creators.

Kalahari, Afar, and Qattara came back to check on their planet and saw that the dinosaurs were causing environmental distress that was destroying the beauty of their Pretty Blue Ball and called an emergency meeting with the other sisters. Qattara lead the meeting. She stated that their father would be very disappointed with the life forms that they had created for the planet Earth. She insisted that the sisters come together to create complex life forms that were worthy of the chi dust that their father entrusted them with. Qattara persuaded Sahara and Sinai to agree that the dinosaurs should be destroyed. Namib supported Chalbi and felt that the dinosaurs should continue to roam the Earth, but the other sisters had decided to no longer contribute their chi dust to producing dinosaurs.

**Chalbi's Voice**

*My sisters and I got into a terrible fight at the planetary development station. My sisters complained that the perfect dinosaur creatures that we had created, and that I adored with all my heart, lived only to eat, breed, and die. They complained that the dinosaurs had no purpose and that they needed no one or nothing to survive. I shamelessly begged and pleaded with my sisters to allow me to keep the dinosaurs. But they all argued that they wanted to design beings that could shape their environment by creating and using their own tools.*

*I thought that this was such a stupid idea when we could continue to make creatures that did not need tools because they could protect themselves with their massive jawbones, claws, tails, teeth, and bodies. The powerful Earth itself would be their shelter and gave them everything that they needed to survive. I could never understand why they would even fathom the thought of creating a being that would be defenseless to the elements of the Earth and all of its other creatures.*

~~~

Chalbi was furious with her sisters for insisting that they eradicate the dinosaurs to make room for trapped souls in dying bodies. Chalbi asked her sisters what they expected her to do with their handsome, bravura creatures that they all had agreed to make. Chalbi was never one to show emotion, especially love or sadness, but she couldn't stop the stalwart tears from falling from her eyes when she asked her sisters, "Where are the dinosaurs supposed to go?" Kalahari avoided making eye contact with Chalbi because she feared that she would be taken in by her tears, she looked away and said, "It should be easy to get rid of them, it's not like they have feelings. They're just big, ugly, stupid beasts who graze and lay eggs, come on Chalbi, you can't be serious."

~~~

Without giving it a single thought, Chalbi reached into the interstellar space in the universe and took a chunk of solar rock from a barely formed planet and hit the Pretty Blue Ball planet with all of her might while screaming, "Awh, I hate you, bitches!" She cracked the Earth's solid landmass into seven pieces. Kalahari, Qattara, and Afar huddled together and sobbed. Sinai and Sahara looked on in disbelief. Namib put her hands around Chalbi's neck, stared deeply into her eyes and said, "Look what you've done to our Pretty Blue Ball," then shoved Chalbi to the floor.

The Jungle Beauty Goddesses stopped speaking to each other at the meeting for millions of years. The lack of communication between the sisters caused a global ice age. The cold breeze from their hearts caused ice sheets and glaciers to spread over the Earth and shrink the tropical forests. They did not speak to each other for millions of years, and the extreme conditions caused over 95% of everything that the Jungle Beauty Goddesses had created to go extinct. Chalbi deeply mourned the loss of her beloved dinosaurs and felt that she could never forgive her sisters for what they had done.

The Jungle Beauty Goddesses snake-dragons were miserable because this was the longest period the sisters had gone without speaking. They came up with a plan to connect themselves into the sacred phrase that the Jungle Beauty Goddesses only shared with each other: "I love you sister. One as the same, the same as one-- without you- there would be none." The snake dragons used their bodies to write this star-lit message into the universe so that each sister could look out into space and see it at the exact same time. A single tear fell from each sister's eye when they saw the message from their snake dragons. They each stopped what they were doing immediately and returned to the planetary development center.

The Jungle Beauty Goddesses hugged each other and then placed their arms in a circle around their planet and hugged and kissed it. Chalbi kneeled on her knees and broke the silence with an apology. She said, "Dear sisters you have allowed me to live my dinosaur dreams for 165 million years. I have been selfish, and I took your love for granted. I am begging for your forgiveness. I am willing to use my chi dust from this moment forward to create more complex beings with grace and gratitude for what you have allowed me to do. Can you please find it in your hearts to forgive me?"

"Of course we forgive you," Sahara said, "But please tell us why you allowed your anger to break your vows and almost destroy our planet? I don't believe that you love dinosaurs more than you love us or our planet. Is there something more that you aren't telling us? What if we had created complex beings with emotion, souls, and karmic contracts? Can we trust that you will never damage the planet again?"

Chalbi had a secret that she never shared with anyone, not even Namib. She was afraid to tell her sisters that the real reason why she never wanted to create complex beings with emotions is because when she was younger, she wanted to believe that she had been lulled by her brother Krishna's flute playing into dancing nude in a lake with other women from another galaxy. She wanted to feel that she had been exploited, victimized, and molested by her brother to feel like a good girl. But she knew in her heart that this was not her truth.

The soul-stirring truth was that her brother Krishna was under Chalbi's spell and she knew that her beauty and charisma caused him to play the flute in the first place. Chalbi learned early in life that real power always lies in the object of one's desire; whatever a being thinks that it is controlling -- is actually controlling them. Chalbi remembers how her brother's eyes were fixated on all of the females perfectly shaped bodies. The graceful moves of their bouncing breasts caused ripples in the lake, but when they stopped dancing there were no more ripples, and Krishna stopped playing his flute. Chalbi realized that day that there were so many more important deeds and affairs that her brother should have been attending to, but he couldn't --because even though he didn't know it— his desire for women controlled his psyche. Chalbi was adamantly against creating complex beings because she knew that they would harm each other in unimaginable ways that would either destroy them or prevent them from reaching their full potential. Controlling a creature's body is always easier than controlling its mind. Chalbi shared this secret with her sisters and said, "Why do you think dinosaurs have small brains?" The Jungle Beauty Goddesses laughed hysterically and focused on restoring life into their planet.

The sisters noticed that Earth's climate had become dry and hot with very little rainfall, after much of the ice glaciers had evaporated. The Pretty Blue Ball planet was a drier, cooler place. Many of the swamps and forests were now replaced with open plains. The coastlines began to shrink, and the sisters could see the deserts that their father named after them. The Jungle Beauty Goddesses had decided to come up with a plan to help the Earth recover from the mass extinction that they had caused before their parents discovered what had happened.

The crack in the Earth caused the atmosphere to become warm and humid. The monsoon conditions created rivers, basins, lakes, new seas, and oceans in the cracks that were continuing to spread further apart. The Jungle Beauty Goddesses noticed that the broken landmass stopped the surviving creatures from roaming the Earth freely and that each of the seven continents began to develop its unique climate.

Sahara and Sinai suggested that they take advantage of the waterways and began to design a new type of life form that they called mammals to fill the land and oceans. They mixed their chi dust together, made more grass, and hummed together as they created pigs, deer, cats, rhinos, dogs, horses, bears, monkeys, and apes. They produced seals, dolphins, whales, manatees, and walrus, and placed them in the oceans.

The Jungle Beauty Goddesses needed to make more changes to the Earth to make it a more hospitable environment where complex being could survive. They blended their chi dust together, said a few magical words, and sprinkled it over the Earth to transform any remaining gigantic creatures on Earth and make them smaller. The sisters knew that Chalbi was sad over the death of the huge dinosaurs, of which many had wings but could never fly due to their massive size. As a gift of truce to their sister Chalbi, the sisters decided to re-encode the dinosaurs DNA so that they would become much smaller and actually be able to use their wings to fly high above the clouds. Chalbi was delighted.

"I will miss the rumbling and shaking of the Earth when the majestic, gigantic dinosaurs roamed the lands and walked the seas. But what I missed most was not being close to my sisters. I will keep my promise and help my sisters create the perfect being that is capable of taking advantage of all of the resources that our Pretty Blue Ball planet has to offer and is able to live in harmony with the other life forms," Chalbi thought to herself as she sipped the last drop of her lavender tea.

# Chapter Four

# The Perfect Being

**Namib's Voice**

*My sisters have agreed among themselves to create life forms that are capable of behaving, planning, and thinking beyond their programmed DNA codes. My sisters are bored by having to monitor the instinctual and predictable behaviors of creatures that are incapable of understanding and expanding the beauty of the planet Earth.*

*Oh, how I wish they would change their minds. I think they are causing us to make an atrocious mistake. Have my sisters even begun to contemplate the complications of creating beings with emotions and the conscious awareness of their own existence?*

*If I am going to agree with this mad idea to develop more complex beings, I must insist that we give them a divine purpose to compensate for the emotional and intellectual abuse that we are unintentionally bestowing upon them.*

*When baby dinosaurs hatched, their parents did what we programmed them to do. They fed their babies the foods that we instructed them to feed them whether it was only leaves, other animals, or both. Many of them hatched and never saw their parents or cared to...many died unbeknownst to their parents. Other creatures ate their carcasses and kept about their business. If we create beings with emotions they will feel as we do about their loved ones.*

*I am afraid that these complex beings will need rules that extend beyond their DNA coding. And who is going to establish these rules for these infantile creatures that possess the powers of gods? Will they be intellectually capable of ruling themselves? The thought of baby-sitting lesser beings will impinge upon the nature of my freedom. If we create a being that needs us, we will no longer be free ourselves. We will be tethered to the boundaries of their fate and the magicians of their dreams.*

*To what degree do we help them navigate and adapt to planet Earth? If we give them the ability to think, should we program their DNA so that we can control what, and how, they think? The more I consider it, the more I am convinced that this is a terrible idea. I think Chalbi was right; dinosaurs are the perfect creatures for Earth.*

*If we give these complex beings the ability to think and learn, they will inevitably want to know who created them and why. Over time they will blame us for their plight on Earth and begin their journey of searching for their creators and demanding answers. Daddy never properly prepared us for the enormous responsibility of developing life forms to populate the planets. He should have skipped the grandiose Deity Ball and spent some quality time teaching my sisters and me about the ultimate purpose of life on planets.*

*Poor Daddy, he let Mother talk him into starting a family. I have always wondered if he would have been happier without us. I am so angry with him for letting his love for Mother override his quest for truth. I love Mother, but a part of me despises her for being so selfish. I have never even seen this woman cry. Does she care about anybody but herself? If she really loves Daddy as much as she proclaims, she should have focused on his greatness, and not tried to burden him with the responsibilities of children.*

*Because my sisters and I are a sibling-set born from the spark of one kiss, we are collectively one being divided into seven personalities. We cannot accurately create without the consensus agreement of all the sisters. If I choose not to participate in developing complex beings and thus nullify the consensus, my sisters will hate me. If this happens, none of us will be happy, and I will have to decide if losing the love of my sisters is worth not creating complex beings for planet Earth. The mere thought of imagining an eternity without the love and friendship of my sisters is painful and unbearable. Now I know how daddy must have felt when mother persuaded him to have children.*

*Tomorrow my sisters and I will meet at our planetary development station to collaborate on our new adventure to create the perfect being. I have made peace within my own soul, and I now know what I need to do to feel complete. I am ready to join my sisters wholeheartedly without reservations. I realize now that my divine purpose throughout eternity is to find a path of happiness and joy that allows me to grow and expand intellectually and spiritually. This will always align me with the collective journey of my sisters. This is who I am. This is why I am here.*

*Now that I understand why I am doing this, the outcome, consequences, and results will never matter to me. I need the camaraderie of my sisters, and taking this journey with them is the only way I will ever be completely happy.*

*These complex beings must have a purpose so that they can ultimately understand why it is necessary to experience the emotions of love, hate, jealousy, happiness, sadness, anger, disappointment, joy, embarrassment, and pain on our planet Earth. Their perfection must be a buried treasure of special gifts and talents developed on planet Earth, lying within the purest desire of their hearts, and only visible through their soul's eye. They will only have access to this treasure by listening to and obeying their souls. Without a reason to exist, they might as well be dinosaurs.*

~~~

The Jungle Beauty Goddesses met in the dome-shaped meeting room and sat around a long rectangle table. The table was covered in a lime green cloth, decorated with purple flowers and purple cups for their lavender tea. Of course no meeting was complete without the manna muffins that the sisters adored. Each sister was required to bring a proposal, contained within a gemstone sphere, that included the qualities, characteristics, physical appearance, and basic nature of the complex beings that they thought were important in creating their new perfect being. After greeting each other with kisses and hugs, Sahara called the meeting to order.
~~~

“The previous creatures that dominated our Pretty Blue Ball were programmed by us to only act on habit and instinct. There was no emotion, intuition, or mental activity that was not encoded in their DNA. The purpose of our meeting today is to develop the perfect being with complex emotions and a sophisticated intellectual capacity that we feel will nurture and cherish our planet Earth, share it unselfishly with other life forms, and have the ability to utilize the natural resources of Earth to expand and evolve beyond the limitations of their DNA coding. If you agree, take a sip of your lavender tea, and raise your cup to the center of the table.”

All seven of the sisters took a sip of their lavender tea and raised their cups.

Qattara volunteered to present her proposal first. She closed her eyes and waved her hands around her garnet gemstone sphere until it created a hologram of a dark purplish-brown baby that began transforming into a being very similar to the Jungle Beauty Goddesses themselves, except having shorter necks. Qattara suggested that they call these being “humans” and that they mold them from the rich soil from the continent of Africa near Kenya. She told her sisters that the beings’ color should be as beautiful as the velvety black space that fills the universe with the dark matter that separates and connects all there is. Qattara explained that they should give their new complex being a physical body that is vulnerable, beautiful, strong, and fragile. The human body should be naked; without feathers, fur, leather, or scales.”

“I think it’s offensive to create beings that look so much like us,” Chalbi says, "At least when I created the dinosaurs I used my imagination. There should always be a clear difference between gods, goddesses, and lesser beings.”

"I thought it would be a compliment to father and mother to design our perfect beings in their image. I didn't mean to be offensive," Qattara answered while looking at her reflection in her lavender teacup.

"This is abusive, Qattara! How would they defend themselves against other life forms, the cold winters, the hot summers, the rainstorms, the snow blizzards? Where will they live, sleep? What will they eat?" Sinai asked while slowly rubbing her forehead.

Afar raised her teacup to Qattara and said, "This is absolutely brilliant. Don't listen to Sinai. We can encode their DNA to give them the ability to create their own homes, clothes, tools, and whatever else they need. We will provide them with all of the resources they need from our planet Earth. If we are serious about creating more complex beings they must have the innate ability to be innovative beings."

Sinai stood up from the conference table and began pacing back and forth, exclaiming, "I think we are making an irreparable mistake. Can we guarantee that each human will have equal access to the resources needed for survival? If we don't give them the resources that they need to survive, our beings will be just like the walking dead. They will always be obsessed with finding their next meal, and wondering where they will lay their heads at night. They will never be able to experience the spontaneous joy of living completely in the moment. I don't like this. I don't like this at all. Why are we creating beings designed merely to exist, suffer, and die?"

Sinai sat back in her chair, took a sip of her lavender tea, took a bite from her manna muffin, and raised her eyebrow to Qattara, who was waiting patiently for Sinai to complete her proposal.

Qattara pursed her lips while straightening her head wrap, looked around the conference table at her sisters and said, "We should give all of the humans the same body shape and size; same skin, eye, and hair color.

And all of their hair should be the same texture and length. We should make sure that all humans have the same nose, lips, and cheekbones down to the smallest detail to ensure that their facial features look one and the same.

If we make them look different, they will inevitably hate each other. They will use their perceived differences as reasons to exploit, oppress, and annihilate each other. I propose that we create a male and a female like our mother and father, who are capable of producing offspring. Additionally, I propose that we encode their DNA to have certain instincts like our other life forms that we have created in the past. For this endeavor to be successful, they must have predictable behaviors that are completely out of their control. Without these instincts they will stop producing other humans, and we will be forced to come up with new ideas for complex beings in the near future."

"How will they be able to tell each other apart? Kalahari asks. "We all look different from each other, and our other siblings and father and mother have managed to love us equally.

Afar quips under her breath, "Yes, but this doesn't necessarily mean that we feel the love equally."

"What type of instincts do you suggest that we encode in their DNA?" Sahara asks.

"One question at a time," Qattara says in a quiet voice, "I have thought about this, and I believe that if we make humans look different without implanting their DNA with the wisdom to honor, cherish, and respect others who do not look the same as themselves; we are setting ourselves up for a potential disaster that could possibly destroy our Pretty Blue Ball. Our parents have wisdom. It is impossible to program wisdom into the DNA of our complex being. We can encode their DNA with the potential for wisdom, but wisdom is an attribute that develops over long periods of time. My concern is that they will destroy themselves before their DNA code for wisdom fully unlocks. This is not a risk that I am comfortable with taking at this point in developing our complex beings.

To answer your question, Sahara, I think that the only instinct that we should give our complex beings is the desire to live even with the knowledge of inevitable death. We will encode their DNA with certain survival muscle reflexes, but the main focus is that we must encode in their species a preservation of life gene that dominates.

Qattara waves her hands over her garnet sphere, and the human image dissipates back like a winding tornado back into the gemstone globe. Sahara stands up and asks the sisters if there are any further questions. The conference room is momentarily filled with silence before Kalahari says, "I would like to go next."

Kalahari waves her hand over her rose quartz crystal sphere and instantly projects a rotation of images that fill the conference room of their parents kissing, all seven sisters sitting on the back of the long black train of their father's robe hugging, giggling, and playing while traveling throughout the galaxy; all seven sisters sipping lavender tea and eating manna muffins, sitting with their mother under the pink ponytail tree by the waterfall; family celebrations, elaborate meals, ceremonies and dances at thousands of their siblings Deity Balls. At the end of Kalahari's presentation, all of the sisters were weeping happy tears. Kalahari said in a loud firm voice to her sisters, "I don't really care what they look like, but if we do not encode them with the capacity to love and develop relationships with their families and friends, we are not making complex beings, we are creating robots that look like us. We must encode them with the ability to feel love.

If we give them the capacity to love, "Chalbi says with a grin, "then we must also give them the capacity to feel hate, jealousy, sadness, and anger. They should experience the same range of emotions that we have. They will never know if they love someone unless that emotion is contrasted with its opposite.

The sisters stood up and clapped after Kalahari's presentation. They each congratulated her for creating a presentation that reminded them of how lucky they are to know of no other existence that does not include love.

The meeting was interrupted by their sister, Kwan Yin, whose tears streamed down her smiling cheeks. She told them that she was deeply moved by Kalahari's presentation. The Jungle Beauty Goddesses gathered around Kwan Yin, each waiting their turn to give her a hug and a kiss. "Father and mother would be so proud of you. I see that you are taking your planetary duties seriously," Kwan Yin said, "Is there any way that I may be of assistance to you?" Chalbi quickly answered, "No, thank you. We have worked through some major obstacles, but at this point, we have finally come to an agreement on what is best for our planet."

Qattara reached out to hold both of Kwan yin's hands and looked directly into her eyes and said, "I love you, sister—thank you for coming, but we are fine. Your planet is so different from ours. Your beings experience constant pain and suffering, and you enjoy bestowing them with mercy and compassion to make them happy. I know that you receive a tremendous amount of pleasure from helping them, but we are looking to create a more independent type of life form which doesn't need us as much."

"We don't know everything there is to know about creating complex life forms," Sahara interjected. "Is there is any advice that you can give us that we may have perhaps overlooked?"

Kwan Yin responded, "Every god and goddess has a different way of viewing the world that he or she chooses to create. There is no wrong or right way to create the perfect being for your planet. However, I will caution you with the wisdom that many of our siblings and I have discovered over time -- Your perfect beings will always believe that they need you to perform miracles for them even when reality begs to differ. They will ultimately blame their creators for all of the misery in their lives, no matter how much you provide for them. You will never do enough. They will never be happy, and they will never be truly grateful. However, you must love them anyway, beyond anything that you have ever loved. Rule your planet with an everlasting sense of compassion and mercy. This is a thankless job.

Let me not forget why I am here; I have actually come to inform you that our parents will be arriving in seven days to assist you in placing your planet Earth back on its orbit for the rest of its eternity." Kwan Yin wished her sisters the best of luck, bowed, and waved good-bye before leaving.

Afar placed her hands on her face, then ran her fingers through her long brunette hair and said, "No, no, no. Why are they coming so soon, we are hardly ready?"

"It's been a few billion years," Chalbi said. "We have been creating life forms for a while."

"Life?—you call creating dinosaurs life?" Kalahari says while rolling her eyes.

"Okay, okay, that's enough. We really need to complete the proposals. Daddy will be so disappointed with us if we are not ready when he gets here." Sahara says. "I'll go next."

Of all the sisters, Sahara looked the most like her father. Diamonds sparkled around her beautiful bald head as she stood to give her presentation. Her stern, regal presence demanded the respect of her sisters. Sahara waved her hands over her lapis lazuli sphere and projected a hologram image of a large brain in the center of the conference table.

"I propose that we create a brain that has unlimited potential to learn, remember, problem-solve, and develop innovative ideas. All of our previous life forms have remained slaves to their environment. They lack the intellectual capacity to think beyond the boundaries of their DNA programming. We should create beings who are capable of thinking logically, who can learn from their mistakes and have the intellectual capacity to become rulers of their fate. We should expand the size of the perfect beings' brain so that it can acquire, store, and retrieve new information and have the ability to pass this knowledge to future generations. No other life form that we have created thus far has had the intellectual capacity to develop their own set of rules and laws beyond the pre-packaged DNA-repertoire of behaviors that we have provided."

We should give them a mind that is so powerful, multifaceted, and brilliant that they will need minimal intervention from us. Why should we make them weak, sniffling, begging, whining creatures who worship us? They will create their own justice and decide for themselves who should be rewarded or punished. In the past, we controlled our beings by predetermining all of their choices. The herbivores ate plants, and the carnivores ate meat because we instructed them to do so. All of our previous life forms mated where and when we told them to. I propose that we create a perfect being and give them free will. Our new sophisticated beings will be designed with an innate ability to construct their own religion, government, and educational institutions. They will be free, and so will we."

"I know this is a silly question," Afar asked, "but hypothetically speaking, do you think they could ever become smarter than us?"

"Sahara, your idea makes me nervous," Chalbi said while fiddling with the ring in her nose. "Is it possible that we could create a being that we could have very little control over, and perhaps they evolve into beings that we fear?"

"If we give them complete free will with unlimited potential-- they could possibly destroy themselves and our Pretty Blue Ball," Namib said.

"I think it is impossible for them ever to be smarter or superior to us. They are our creation living off the resources of our planet. Their physical and mental power will never transcend beyond the boundaries of Earth's gravity" Sahara said.

"I got it! I got it!" Chalbi shouted. "I know how to ensure that their intellectual powers never exceed ours— we will make sure that they die. Death. Yes, sweet death will be the factor that reigns supreme over their physical destiny. We will torture them-- I mean subdue them-- with the knowledge of their own demise and that of their loved ones. Death will be the one common trait that all humans will share with all other life forms. If they never die, they will never grow, change, or evolve because there would be no reason to.

An impending sense of non-existence will make them humble. Like Qattara suggested, we will instruct their DNA to fight for and value a life that will be ultimately taken from them. But the most powerful controlling factor is that we will bestow them with the ability to love each other as Kalahari suggested—deeply, intensely, and unconditionally; yet they will be forced to helplessly watch their loved ones die, not knowing if they will ever see them again. No matter how big their brain is, no matter how much knowledge they have, no matter how strong they are—we would never have to worry about them rebelling against us because they will know that their time on Earth is limited. We should not use death as a mechanism for punishment and reward.

Humans should die at various points in their life cycle for a multitude of reasons, otherwise impeding death would become predictable, and this will decrease its sobering effect on their psyche. If our perfect beings are to maximize their time on Earth they must learn to welcome death as a

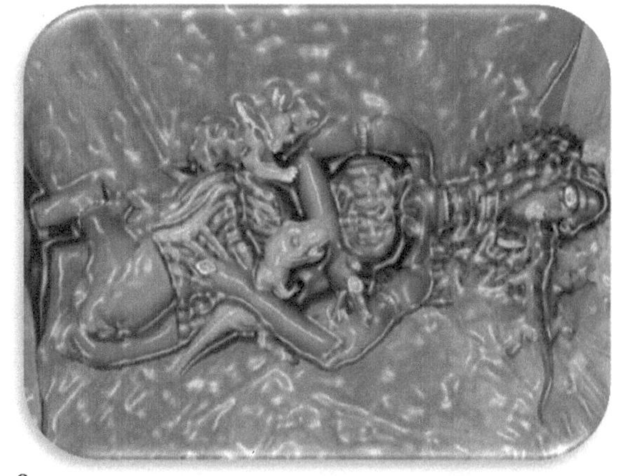

transformation. Only death will motivate them to live a rich and meaningful life truly. The conscious awareness of their impending death will cause them to re-think every decision they encounter. They will aim to eliminate conditions, circumstances, and possibly other beings that make their limited time on Earth more painful than it has to be. Death will inspire them to cherish their own life and the others which they hold dear in their hearts. This is my contribution to our perfect being. Sorry nothing will emerge from my tiger's eye sphere ball. I hadn't thought much about how I would contribute until this moment; please accept this as my official proposal."

"If we give them free-will, they ultimately can kill themselves," says Qattara. "But in order to prevent this we must make sure that the survival life force instinct is the most potent genetic building block. Without this our plan will not be successful, and our planet will be replete with unsophisticated life forms.

"I am worried that they will fear death and then ultimately fear living," Sinai said. "But I respect your reasoning behind why it is important that our perfect beings must die, Chalbi. We as goddesses never die, and I don't want to even try to imagine what my existence would be like without my family. It seems cruel, but necessary for beings on planet Earth. Well, I guess I will go next." Sinai waves her hand over her emerald sphere and hologram images of her project onto the table, one by one of her engaged in various artistic activities. In one image Sinai is star-sking from galaxy to galaxy, on a pair of aquamarine skies, leaving long trails of wavy, sparkling, colorful stardust behind her. In the next image, Sinai performs a slow graceful, elegant, seductive dance on a waxing and waning moon, where at moments she appears to be making love to it—and it to her--and then the moon comes to life and becomes her dance partner. Sinai slides down the inside of the shifting crescent-shaped moon, and then she twirls inside of both tips, then it fades into the next image. Sinai playfully juggles 23 small planets, as she moves her neck around in a circle, then she lines them up in the shape of a helix that winds up and down her body until each one disappears. More artistically beautiful images of Sinai fill the room with her painting, sculpting, drawing, playing instruments, singing and meditating. After all, of her life-size hologram images gracefully dissipate back into Sinai's emerald sphere, she began to speak. "The one gift that I would like to give our perfect beings is the thing that I cherish most about being a goddess. I would like to give them the joy of spontaneity, having fun, being playful, and living in the moment. I want them to find something to do that gives them a sense of timelessness; without this, they are just things made of flesh. I want them to have a sense of lightheartedness and freedom of self-expression that only thrives in the moment of time. I know this isn't as fancy or complicated as what the rest of you have presented, but I think it would be a wretched existence for our perfect beings if they are compounded only with matters of life and death. Something should saturate their spirit with excitement, joy, and unconditional pleasure. There should be something that they do with their own bodies that causes them to fall madly in love with their own life. I think we owe them a sense of happiness that can only be fulfilled from living in the moment of their own being."

The Jungle Beauty Goddesses all agreed to include Sinai's suggestions in creating the perfect being without hesitation. Afar hugged Sinai and kissed her on the forehead before standing to present next. "Oh, I think Sinai's idea is absolutely lovely. However, I feel that they should be able to create whatever they want, not just babies and dancing on the moon. We should make them creative beings that are capable of designing the type of world that they want to live in. They should have powers similar to daddy's. Why should he have all the fun and what not? You know how we created nests for the birds, caves for the bears, and trees for monkeys? I think we have done a great job making them beautiful with all types of designs, feathers, scales, and fur to keep them warm and cold. We have instructed every creature that we have invented thus far where to live, how to live, and what to look like. Wouldn't it be a great idea if we programmed our perfect being to create its own home, give it the ability to decide how it wants to cover its flesh and feet, or even leave it bare for that matter? They should invent what they want to sleep and sit on, create and cook their own food, and decide who they want to procreate with or not at all. They should fix their own hair, do what they want, and use the planet Earth's resources as their creative toolbox. Ooh and maybe some nice jewelry and whatever else they need within the boundaries of Earth's gravitational laws? Why give them such a big oh brain, if we don't intend for them to use it? I would love to see what they come up with on their own. We might be surprised and fascinated by their creations. I mean, they can't possibly hurt themselves. We know everything there is to know about Earth, there's nothing here that could hurt them to the point where they would destroy themselves. This would be so much fun to watch. Well, that's all I want to say." Afar took a sip of her lavender tea, ran her fingers through her long dark brown hair, smiled, and said, "Namib, honey, I think you are next. I am ready to put this project behind me so I can get back to my life."

Sahara gave Afar a stern admonishment, saying, "Creating life for Earth is now your life. You cannot keep running around from galaxy to galaxy as if you have no responsibilities. You are no longer a goddette. You are a goddess, and we expect your full participation in monitoring and protecting our planet Earth. Your selfish foolishness must stop now. Your behavior is unbecoming of the daughter of the supreme being."

Afar responded, "Well, you ladies would never begin to understand how I feel because you see your own beauty reflected to you in the likeness of father and mother, and in the velvety dark energy and black matter of the universe. I don't feel like I belong here, and if I could have chosen my eternal existence, it surely would not have been here where I look like some odd, colorless, being from another universe. You say you love me-- but do you love me because you have to--- or because you want to? I want to know what it is like to feel loved by another being, not because he created me, but because he selected me. I'll tell you what; if I could have created myself, I would look like my siblings of the same birth set. But this is the hand that I have been dealt, and obviously father knows best, so I don't want to waste another moment of our time complaining. Namib, honey, we are all waiting for you."

Namib waves her hand, round her Amethyst crystal globe. A piercing, violet, blue flame emerges and hovers in the middle of the table. Moments later, several bodies of various sizes and shapes envelop the flame before morphing into another being. In each new body, the violet-blue flame becomes brighter and more beautiful than the one before. Next, this violet-blue flame then turns into crystal-like liquid drops that saturate the room. It then turns into the shape of a single prospective human, who looks deeply into each goddess's eyes, and then gently smiles before shrinking back into a flame inside of Namib's Amethyst sphere. Namib blew out the flickering flame in her crystal sphere before she began to speak.

"We must give them a soul, something that extends beyond time and space. A being will never evolve into a more intricate way of thinking or believing if every aspect of its existence dies. There must be a part of the perfect being that retains the lessons learned from each lifetime after the physical body dies. I propose that we give our perfect being an eternal soul that has the capacity to take on the personality and physical likeness of each incarnation of its new body. We will give each soul a special talent or ability that can only be expressed, developed, and mastered on the planet Earth. The purpose of life will be to discover and cherish what is directly in front of them.

If the perfect beings are not given an opportunity to come back to Earth to apply their new levels of knowledge, skill, and wisdom, they will never have a chance to experience the consequences of their actions. Each soul should contain a specific talent that unfolds during each incarnation. The degree to which this talent unfolds will be based on the being's ability to align with its own truth. This truth is the coalescence of both: all the power there is, and the lessons of each lifetime for an individual soul. Our perfect beings will align their loyalty to the maintenance and stability of our planet Earth because it will be the only home that allows their souls to experience different parts of themselves. Otherwise, why would they care about a planet that they will never experience again or only experience in the same manner repeatedly? For example, wouldn't it be interesting if Mother and Father could exchange places and see the universe from the other's perspective? As goddesses we are, in essence, lifeless beings because we cannot die. As such, we are eternally fixated in one reality, which limits our opportunities for growth; and therefore we cannot expand our conscious awareness beyond anything other than who we are at this moment.

I utterly despise our brother Dionysus. He was given the planet Eniw where he created beings who are intoxicated, lustful, and corrupt, savages. But what if I had an opportunity to be born with his body, and to see and experience the universe from his perspective? Maybe I wouldn't hate him at all. In fact, I may or may not have made the same choices. But how will I ever truly know or understand his perspective? Maybe wine and lust are neither good nor bad, but I can't determine this because I will always be me in the same body planted forever in time. In order for our perfect being to be sophisticated and complex in its ability to think and problem-solve, we must give it eternal life beyond the demise of its physical body."

"This is preposterous! Chalbi shouts, "We killed my dinosaurs because of this crazy idea about creatures who change bodies and live forever?"

"Namib, this has never been done before by gods and goddesses. Only Daddy and Mother have the power to create eternal life," says Qattara.

Namib responded, "I have a plan that I am convinced is going to work, though I am not sure if we will be able to control all of the outcomes. When we design the DNA code for the perfect being and mix it with the star powder paste and the chi dust that our parents gave us at the Deity Ball, we should then stir in an elixir of saliva from mother and father when they kiss. Our parent's saliva is the mystical potion that will give our perfect beings a soul and eternal life."

Addressing her controversial sister, Sinai exclaimed, "I think you have absolutely lost your mind, Namib. Maybe you hate Dionysus because he rivals the depths of your own immortality."

Jumping on the bandwagon, Kalahari added, "You sound insane Namib, how could you fathom the thought of betraying the trust and love of our parents. I am not comfortable with this idea. It feels evil."

Namib begged, "No listen, Kalahari, these perfect beings will have soul mates who will love them throughout eternity, just the way you and I love each other. They will support each other, while in different roles and bodies, during several lifetimes. How will they learn to love if we only give them one chance at love? Please sisters; I beseech your support in this endeavor. If we do not give them a purpose for the pain and suffering that a diminishing physical life on Earth will inflict upon them; they will be nothing but aimless beasts, roaming the Earth waiting to die. This is not what we want."

"I find your idea quite intriguing," said Sahara, "I think that we all can come to some sort of agreement if we set some boundaries for our perfect beings. Maybe it's not a bad thing that Chalbi broke the landmass into seven continents. What we will do is create our perfect beings on the continent of Africa where it is warm, and the food is plentiful. They won't need to worry about attire to protect them from harsh weather conditions. They will all have dark skin that can easily absorb the sun rays with very little, if any variation, in their facial features between the males and females, as we previously discussed. We will give them coarse short hair that requires very little maintenance. They do not have wings, and surely they cannot swim for long distances, so they will be confined to one geographical location on the planet. We will monitor them periodically, and they will have babies, eat fish, pick the berries off the trees and live happily ever after. Our parents will be here shortly, and we need to move swiftly on this project."

"I think it's a marvelous idea. How do you plan to extract this spittle from mother and father?" Afar asks.

"Mother and father can barely keep their hands off each other, so it won't be hard," Kalahari laughed.

When their parents, Dematter and Nebula, arrived at the planetary development station to put the planet Earth back onto its orbit position, the daughters presented them with roses. Dematter and Nebula kissed and hugged their daughters. True to form, they then passionately kissed each other. The spittle from their kiss dripped onto the roses that they were still holding. When Dematter and Nebula placed their roses on the conference table, the Jungle Beauty Goddesses took the roses and poured the sweet juices from their kiss into the mixture of the perfect being and planted it into the earth to blossom once the planet had been set back on its orbit.

The Jungle Beauty Goddesses sat in a circle around the Pretty Blue Ball on the back of the long, magnificent, trains of Dematter and Nebula's robe as they glided through the universe. The planet prop was removed, and Earth was placed back onto its orbiting space in the universe. After accompanying their parents on the interstellar journey to the Milky Way Galaxy, the Jungle Beauty Goddesses would return to the planetary development station periodically to monitor the progress of their beings on planet Earth.

The Jungle Beauty Goddesses were exhausted from developing life forms for their planet. They all agreed to take a break and meet up in a few million years at the planetary development station to check on their humans – their perfect beings.

## Chapter Five

# Earth Laws

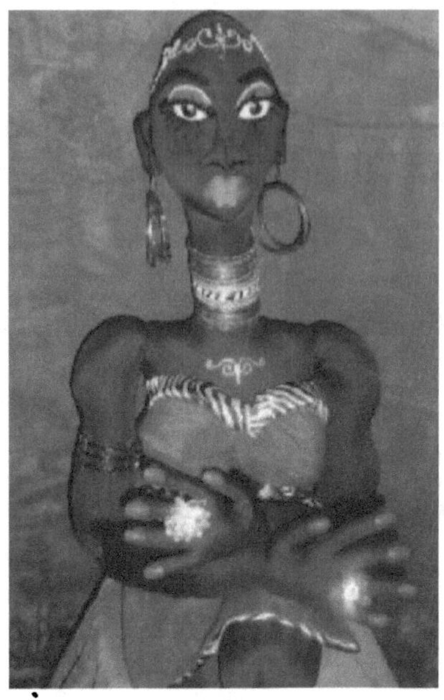

**Sahara's Voice**

*The last time I saw my sisters was approximately 200,000 years ago. We parted ways after placing planet Earth back on its orbit with Father and Mother. It had been such a delightful time for me, though I really needed a break from all of the "perfect creature" and "complex being" drama.*

*I find it amusing that my siblings frequently ask me why I have chosen to be a bald woman. I find hair to be a ridiculous waste of time. You style it one day, and the next day, it needs to be styled again. Who has time for such utter foolishness? I don't care about what's on the head; I care about what's in the head—and there appears to be nothing inside of my sisters' heads but sheer foolishness.*

*My sisters don't seem to comprehend the logic that one can never control any being that has a mind of its own. As soon as humans realize that they cannot avoid death, they will be relentless in their desire to rule the planet Earth. They will quickly learn that there is absolutely no point in fighting for something that does not belong to them. But they will truly become wise when they realize that their lives are not worth living unless they are willing to die for something.*

*The humans who are the first to understand how the Earth game is played will destroy the lives of others. They'll destroy the lives of those who are willing to do anything to have one more day to spend with a loved one, watch a sunset, or listen to the birds sing. I pity the humans who will learn to value and cherish the breath in their bodies. Holding on to this ever diminishing breath will cause them to suffer unimaginable indignities by other humans who have welcomed and befriended death. What have we done?*

*Thoughts, beliefs, and attitudes are more powerful than any other entity because they create and alter a beings perception of reality. A being will never be more than what it is capable of conceiving in its own mind. The invisible realm of the mind is where everything imaginable first originates. Every goal, dream, plan, idea, or action was first a simple thought that became more complex and convoluted over time.*

*We gave our humans the ability to think. They are capable of analyzing their past and pondering their future. This worries me a little bit, but since my sisters and I have gone out of our way to keep them physically satisfied, this should keep them mentally complacent and not cause of any trouble.*

*My sisters and I have an urgent dinner meeting with our parents tomorrow evening to discuss the progress of planet Earth and its life forms. I feel little guilty because my sisters and I have not been back to the planetary development station to check on our complex beings to see how they have adjusted to planet Earth for almost 200,000 years. I don't understand why daddy seems to be so distressed. We did everything that was expected from us, maybe even more than our elder siblings have done for their planets.*

*We took it upon ourselves to create beings that for the most part-- do not need hand-holding and assistance from a higher being. We gave them free will and the ability to think for themselves. We provided a safe place for them to live with all the food and natural shelter that they would ever need- in a perfect climate. We made sure that they could only remain in one geographical location on the planet and designed all of the beings to look physically similar so that there would be no divisive issues to bring about conflict.*

*Humans have a lot of geographical space so that they would not encroach on the ecosystem of other life forms. We programmed their DNA to bring about a natural death at a time that their physical bodies could no longer participate fully in Earth activities so that no one would become a burden to another being beyond his years of usefulness. We put in plenty of natural resources and set up measures to prevent overpopulation.*

I think daddy is bored and he misses us very much. Why can't he just come out and admit that he misses his baby girls. Oh no! I know why daddy really wants to meet with my sisters and me tomorrow—him and mother --- No. No. No. We have new siblings. I know that is what it is. They promised us that they wouldn't have any more children. Sweet blazing stars, another deity ball to attend. I can't believe that they could even contemplate the thought of loving any children more than my sisters and I. Being the youngest is such a coveted position in a family. I loved being coddled by our older siblings and adored by our parents. I am absolutely devastated. I must warn my sisters to prepare them for the downward shift in status in daddy's and mother's hearts. I can't believe that I have the audacity to feel jealousy. How silly and illogical of me.

~~~

The Jungle Beauty Goddesses had agreed to meet at their favorite garden in the courtyard, where they waited for their mother prior to taking their vows at their Deity Ball. The dinner meeting with their parents was scheduled for much later on that evening. This would give them a chance to catch up on the details of each other's lives since placing their planet back on its orbit. They were unable to contact Afar to inform her about the meeting, but it was not unlike her to immerse herself in some bizarre interstellar activities in faraway galaxies.

The courtyard was more beautiful than they remembered. The majestic, thick tall trees with pink heart-shaped leaves were plush and thick, and the bright yellow rose bushes surrounded the lavender lake with cascading layers of rainbow colored waterfalls. The iridescent white opal benches that surrounded the lake were encircled by various shades of baby blue tulips that grew from the thick pink grass. The garden air smelled like whiffs of fresh-cut lime.

When the Jungle Beauty Goddesses arrived, 6 glasses of cold lavender tea with spruces of mint leaves and a platter filled manna muffins waited for them on the shimmery pink opal table. The sisters arrived at the garden within moments of each other. They shrieked with laughter and joy as they hugged and kissed each other while jumping up and down. The sisters held up their glasses to toast their success of developing a planet that their parents would be proud of and for creating complex beings that did not pester them through prayer and worship with the task
~~~

of making their lives bearable. In unison they said, "I love you sister. One as the same, the same as one-- without you- there would be none." They toasted their glasses together and proceeded to sit three each on two opal benches facing each other.

"I haven't had the chance to check on Earth since the day that we accompanied mother and father to place it back on its orbit. Chalbi said while fiddling with her nose ring after taking a sip of the lavender tea. Qattara and I came in third in an intergalactic star-ski competition that required a tremendous level of commitment and dedication. We thought about checking on the planet, but we assumed that one of you would drop by the planetary development station. I also visited a planet where the beings physically die, but they can choose to come back to life in 10 year intervals. In order to live in their physical bodies forever they must choose to die at 3 points in their life. Parents can select one 10-year-death for a child from birth to ten. If they choose not to participate they will die permanently at the age of 25 years old. You would not believe the vast and complicated life cycles that exist throughout the universe. These beings have developed a culture around where the bodies must be stored until they come back to life, as well as, many educational institutions that teach them how to adapt to the changes that have taken place over the ten years that they were gone.

Many of the beings are traumatized by the fact that their bodies have aged the 10 years that they were dead, and they hardly recognize their community, family, or friends. I don't understand the logic behind this life and death pattern. I have never seen or heard of anything like this before. In fact, it is a very strange existence. The death of the dinosaurs has changed my perspective about life and death in ways that I am still unable to articulate. Enough about my galaxy travels; when was the last time any of you checked on our Pretty Ball planet?"

"I was on the planet Niarb on the Intergalactic Research Committee working to create a method whereby beings from every planet would be capable of speaking a universal language," Sahara interjected. But since language is a cognitive tool that is symbolically reflective of a subjective reality, we wonder if beings from billions of galaxies apart would have anything to talk about. They could perhaps learn about each other's cultures, but would they even want to given the extensive differences that make up their consciousness? Perhaps only the intellectually elite from each galaxy could make some sort of arrangement. I am sorry, Sahara said, I didn't mean to bore my lovely sisters with the sordid details of my galaxy travel. To answer your question, no, I have not checked on our planet, but I am not concerned. We set up proper provisions so that our beings would not need to be monitored by us. Kalahari, did you have a chance to check on planet Earth?"

"I didn't get a chance either; I was so busy. I spent a lot of time comparing and contrasting planets and galaxies with various gender types. Some planets only have the masculine or feminine gender; some have beings that change into the opposite gender at scheduled points in their lives; some beings are a combination of both masculine and feminine energy, and some beings are genderless. The Intergalactic Research Committee that I am on is trying to determine the nature of love and whether it is necessary for a being to be happy. I am so delighted about what we are discovering about emotions, love, sex, and relationships," Kalahari said in her usual high-pitched, animated tone.

"Well, is there anything interesting that you want to share with us," Chalbi asked.

"Well, is there anything interesting that you want to share with us," Chalbi asked.

"Only that those relationships with either lot of sex or no sex at all are the happiest. We haven't figured out why yet," Kalahari answers. "Oh I am sorry, I had planned to check on our planet, but Aphrodite, Brigit, and I visited a galaxy where beings did not have any physical contact with other beings, but there was some type of electric charge in the atmosphere that caused waves of instantaneous neuronal climaxes. We were completely exhausted when we left. I wish you could have been there. It was an amazing experience.

"I also did some work with the Intergalactic Research Committee, where we were looking at the possibility of beings from different galaxies falling in love and the practicalities of how these types of relationships would work. One of things that we are discovering is that this emotional chemical of love is a dangerous unpredictable elixir. When the chemical energies between two beings coalesce, a new energy emerges to create new life forms. We have not been able to control or predict these outcomes."

"Kalahari, that sounds interesting," Namib says to Kalahari, as she exposed her face by gently placing her golden, curly locks behind her ear. "I had almost completely forgotten about my planetary duties. I volunteered at the Karmic Transformation Center, helping the angels, ascended masters, spiritual guides and teachers. We were helping souls select their families, dreams, goals, talents, and gifts before incarnating a new body. We also counseled souls on the mistakes they had made in their prior lives and how to apply lessons learned in their next lives. Some souls wanted to experience two conflicting life circumstances, though that could not occur because the opposite effect of one was needed to shape that of the other.

For example, if they wanted to build their wealth from the ground up, they would need to experience poverty, debt, or financial struggle so that their souls could recognize and cherish its opposite. Most decided that they would rather live a mediocre life with neither extremes of scarcity on the one hand, or abundance on the other hand. Those who wanted to know what it felt like to be free while bound inside of a carcass needed to be physically enslaved. Otherwise there was no other way for the soul to expand and grow. Without these experiences there is only nothingness. Namib explained while fluffing her Mohawk with her fingers. Not only did I not check on our planet, I never planned to. I said from the very beginning that I did not want to create beings that need to be baby-sat. The lessons that they need to learn are best discovered without interference from us because it alters their destiny.

"Sinai, what did you do this summer," Namib asked. "You have been so quiet since we got here. Is everything okay? Namib asked while placing her hand on Sinai's hand and searching for direct eye contact with her. Sinai's eyes looked blankly at her sisters as if she was trying to hide something.

"That reminds me," Kalahari says, "while working on the Intergalactic Love Committee, I heard a vicious rumor that you were having an affair with a Mr. Moon Man Lover. It sounded ridiculous. Don't worry Sinai; I defended your honor. You would never bring shame of this nature to Daddy and Mother. Aphrodite has embarrassed Daddy enough for all of us. Did you have a chance to check on the planet?

"I spent most of my time watching the stars explode and using the stardust to paint new fascinating, colorful, artistic designs throughout the universe, Sinai said. Thank you for defending my honor. I didn't check on our planet. Please accept my apologies. Qattara, what about you?

"I am afraid that Daddy and Mother are going to be extraordinarily disappointed with all of us, Qattara said while tracing her voluptuous red lips with her middle finger as if she were applying invisible lipstick. She then straightens her head-wrap with both hands, tightly clasps her fingers together and rests her chin on top of her folded hands, before nervously beginning to speak. We can't find Afar, and none of us, including myself, have bothered to check on our complex life forms and planet Earth. What if our complex beings needed us? We gave them the ability to love, to think, to feel and then we abandoned them on a strange planet. We don't even know if the changes we made had an adverse effect on their DNA coding, or if the crops came in on time as we designed them to do. We don't know if they cried out for us to help them, and if so, whether their prayers were answered. We don't even know if they are still alive," Qattara said while trying to wipe away a tear inconspicuously. "Daddy trusted us, and we have let him down. We have acted like goddettes instead of goddesses. Our first and foremost responsibility was supposed to be the planet that was given to us for our birthday. We broke our vow to, 'to forsake all others and dedicate and commit our lives to developing, nurturing, and protecting the Pretty Blue Ball, planet Earth, and all of its beings big and small until the death of its Sun.' I am ashamed of us, Qattara said as tears streamed down her cheeks.

Sahara sat next to Qattara and wiped away her tears before kissing each cheek. Trust me; she said to Qattara, loud enough for all of her sisters to hear, "There is absolutely no way that there could be a problem with our planet Earth. Our complex life forms are physically incapable of leaving the region where we created them. We didn't stay away for very long; we were gone less than 200,000 years. We didn't check on our planet for millions of years when dinosaurs roamed the earth. They were huge ferocious creatures, and they did not destroy our planet. What could the naked puny humans possibly do to our planet?

We have stabilized the seasonal cycles that effect agriculture. Unless our complex life forms are as intelligent as we are—which is impossible since we made them -- we have nothing to worry about. The other sisters joined in to console Qattara with kisses, hugs, and telling her that everything was fine.

While they were all so close together, Sahara thought this was the perfect time to tell her sisters why she believed that her parents had called them together for an "urgent dinner meeting."

"I have a secret to tell you," Sahara said in a hushed tone. I am almost sure I know why Mother and Father called us together for dinner this evening." The other sisters gasped with relief.

Qattara says, "You mean you have been resting on your laurels and holding secrets from us while I am tortured with guilt and humiliation?

"No," Sahara says, "I don't know for sure, but I have given it a lot of thought, and I think that the reason our parents want to have a dinner meeting is because they want to be the first to tell us that they are having more children.

"That is the most ludicrous thing I have ever heard," Chalbi said. They promised us that we would be the last siblings.

Kalahari thought aloud, "Daddy doesn't have room left in his heart to love another child after us. I am sorry; I didn't mean for anyone to hear that."

"I wouldn't mind being a big sister," Qattara said. "It would be nice to be able to teach and be looked up to.

"You mean the way we cracked our planet into seven pieces, created, then annihilated, the dinosaurs, and created complex life forms that we failed to check up on? We are perfect role models. Chalbi said, making herself laugh so hard that she could hardly breathe.

Sahara laughed, "We are experts at teaching them about what not to do."

Well, one thing we know for sure is that Daddy and Mother cannot keep their hands off each other.

"They have always been insanely in love", Sinai says. "I think we should show our parents deference. Maybe it will be good for us to have younger siblings. Maybe we will be forced to act more mature and be more responsible with our goddess duties.

I feel a little sad about this, but why dwell on things that we cannot control? After dinner, we should all meet at the Planetary Development Station to check on our planet," Namib says.

The six sisters walked from the courtyard garden to their parent's mansion holding hands and laughing and talking both about everything and nothing at all.

When they arrive at the mansion, their mother, Nebula greets them at the door. She grabs her daughters one by one and kisses them on their forehead, and then on each cheek. Nebula hugged them so tight that she could feel their beating hearts. "I love you so much; Momma loves you so much," she whispered into each daughter's ear. "I love you too, Mother", each daughter said back to her, sounding as if they had stepped back in time to when they were little girls.

The Jungle Beauty Goddesses had forgotten about how much they loved their mother until, while hugging her, they inhaled her scent of sandalwood, frankincense, and rose petals. This fragrance brought back all of their wonderful childhood memories, like watching the stars transition from birth to death as they drank lavender tea and ate manna muffins with their mother. They followed their mother's long, lavish royal purple dress-train into the dining lounge room where their father was waiting for them.

When the Jungle Beauty Goddesses saw that they were having dinner in the Chrysocolla room, they knew that the nature of the dinner was a very serious matter indeed. The room was one of the most beautiful rooms in the palace. The Chrysocolla gemstone floor was a dark, rich, effervescent teal color, with swirls of blazing royal blue, various shades or Earth green, with speckled dashes of golden copper. The oval-shaped dinner table was made of chrysocolla as well, surrounded by a plush, rich, elegant teal u-shaped couch with vibrant royal blue, square pillows, accented by deep gold, fancy, round pillows.

The grand, dazzling, purple amethyst chandelier with sparkling diamonds hung from the dome-shaped ceiling. The surrounding sheer u-shaped amethyst window revealed the silky black universe with multiple shapes and sizes of dancing, twinkling, colorful stars, with lavish splashes of pink, blue, and green haze leisurely drifting by. Curly whiffs of frankincense smoke trails complimented the soft teal light that filled the room.

The golden chalices sitting on the long oval-shaped chrysocolla table were decorated with aquamarine, ruby, and lapis lazuli gemstones and filled with honeysuckle wine. The matching soup bowls were filled with their father's favorite soup made of sunflower, star anise, and basil. Tall purple candles encircled with gold, and purple flowers were beautifully placed in the center of the chrysocolla table.

When the Jungle Beauty Goddesses walked into the room laughing and talking, their father walked over to greet them and gave them a humongous hug that enveloped the six of them together and took in a deep mournful, long, sighs as if he was saying good-bye forever. They all proceeded to their seats for wine and soup. Dematter and Nebula sat in the curve of the u-shaped couch separated only by the robes that they were wearing. Chalbi, Qattara, and Sahara sat across the table from Kalahari, Namib, and Sinai.

Per tradition, they ate dinner in silence. Tranquility is the force that allowed their senses to listen to the sweet sound of nothingness; absorb the mystique of the atmosphere, and savor the taste of their food. Talking would disrupt the delicacy of the moment, and not a single word was uttered until the last sunflower petal had been eaten by everyone. Kalahari broke the silence after everyone had finished eating with an announcement.

She carefully placed her gold spoon encrusted with gemstones in her bowl, burst into a grin, and said, "Daddy, I know why you called us here for this dinner meeting. You and mother don't have to worry, my sisters and I have done a lot of souls searching, shed a few tears, but we are completely over it. We discussed it right before dinner, and we have accepted the fact that you and mother are having more children."

"You and Mother are blissfully, passionately, and intensely in love with each other; it was only a matter of time before you would want to have more children," Sinai says, "I am kind of looking forward to a planning a new Deity Ball."

Sahara says, "It's only logical that you and Mother would continue to produce offspring to help maintain the ever-expanding universe with billions of galaxies and trillions of planets."

Qattara traces her lips with her middle finger, rests her chin on her folded fingers, and replies in a soft tone, "Although we live forever, it's not like we can fall in love and have children, someone has to expand the family."

"Qattara would you rather live for only a short period of time if it gave you the opportunity to experience the feeling of being in love and motherhood or would you rather live forever and never experience the joy of falling in love and parenthood?" Namib asked.

"ENOUGH!" Dematter bellowed. "This is not why we are here."

Their father rarely raised his voice when talking to them. They stopped talking immediately and gave him their full attention. In unison, they said together, "Sorry father." Nebula reached over to hold Dematter's face in her hands and softly kissed him on the lips. She looked directly into his eyes and said, "Dem, please be gentle with them." He whispered back, "you're right."

"Your planet is in dire trouble and is in danger of ceasing to exist in any given moment due to unnatural causes," Dematter says while holding Nebula's hand in a calm, serious tone.

"Daddy, I know you have been under a lot of stress lately. And truthfully, your heart has never healed after the beings on----- Lleh attempted to kill Sesuj. With all due respect, I think you are nervous and overreacting," Namib responded.

"Oh Father," Kalahari pleaded, "there has been a terrible mistake. It is literally impossible for our planet to be in danger of being destroyed. We got rid of the monstrous dinosaurs and replaced them with small complex beings that are incapable of flying or traveling to far distances. They are naked and would die if they were exposed to harsh weather conditions. We placed them on the continent of Africa, where you named the deserts after us for safekeeping. We gave them all the food and shelter they would ever need, and designed the perfect climate so that they would have no need to leave the region where we planted them."

"What information do you have that would lead you and mother to believe that Earth is in endanger of extinction?" Sahara asked.

"Your brother, Maru's planet Mars shares the same sun as your planet Earth. He informed your father and me that his planet is no longer receiving enough radiation from the sun to heat his planet because Earth is retaining more than its fair share of energy. He has noticed that within the last 200 years, over 70 percent of his life forms have perished. Maru's planet is quickly becoming barren and lifeless," Nebula said.

"Mother, this doesn't make sense to me. Given the vastness of space and our planets are billions of miles apart, how could planet Earth be responsible for the death of the beings on Mars?" Sinai asked.

"The land, oceans, and plants are designed to absorb roughly 70% of the sun's radiation to keep your planet Earth warm. The other 30% of the sun's heat is supposed to be reflected back into outer space via ice caps, glaciers, and clouds. It appears that more sun energy is being retained by planet Earth, and less sun energy is going back out into outer space to be recycled in its orbit and shares with other planets. Earth's climate is out of balance. It is believed that your complex human beings are engaged in detrimental activities that are trapping the sun's radiation from dispersing properly from its surface.

The other component is that the protective ozone layer has been damaged by unnatural chemicals so that it is unable to filter out the harsh UV-Rays from the sun to prevent them from penetrating through the Earth's stratosphere. Therefore, your planet Earth is overheating, and your brother Maru's planet is freezing," Dematter explained.

"I don't believe this. I think Maru is jealous and envious that our planet is bigger and more attractive than his. Nothing is ever good enough for him. He is never happy. From the moment he selected his planet, all he has ever done was complain," said Chalbi.

"Your father and I have met him at the planetary development station, and we know that your brother is telling the truth." Nebula said.

"This is ridiculous!" Chalbi shouted. "Maybe if you and Daddy weren't making out, then just maybe the both of you would have been paying attention, and you would have 'PROPERLY' placed planet Earth back on its orbit… if there is the tiniest bit of truth to this nonsense."

"You are completely out of line, young lady! You will apologize at once." Nebula hissed in a soft, low, stern voice.

"I will not apologize, mother!" Chalbi cried, "I have had it up to here." She stood up and placed her hand over her head. "I have been through so much pain and angst developing life forms for that flimsy planet. How is it possible that naked, puny little things without wings, tails, or fangs destroy a planet? If the dinosaurs didn't destroy the planet, there is absolutely no way in the universe that humans could begin to harm it. I can't take much more of this. I didn't choose this existence with these unreasonable, overwhelming duties to develop and nurture a planet that I didn't make. I am sick of it!" Chalbi screamed and sat down in a huff and began to sob. Qattara gently pulled her sister to her bosom and stroked her hair as she cried uncontrollably. "It's okay Chalbi." Qattara whispered to her repeatedly until she was emotionally capable of sitting up to rejoin the conversation.

The Jungle Beauty Goddesses knew that that the depth of Chalbi's tears extended well beyond their parent's accusations. Chalbi's heart had never quite healed from their agreement to kill all off the dinosaurs in order to create beings that could help take care of the planet Earth. Dematter and Nebula were stunned at Chalbi's reaction. Although she had a quick wit and dry humor about her, Chalbi was never a rebellious daughter prior to working at the planetary development station. Chalbi's disrespectful display of anger towards her parents was out of character for her.

Sahara stood up and said, "Father and Mother, I think I speak for all of us…we stand by our sister, Chalbi. We have worked very hard on this endeavor with very little help from anyone. We took proper provisions to create complex beings who could adapt to our planet without begging and whining for assistance to meet all of their needs. I have faith in the enormous amount of planning that my sisters and I put into this project and that all is well. I assure you that there has been some type of misunderstanding." Sahara's eyes searched around the table, and each sister glared back into her eyes a fierce, silent oath of agreement. After everything they had been through together, not even the love of their parents could scratch the surface of the bond that they had established while developing their planet Earth.

Silence permeated the room before Dematter stood up to speak. The mood was now somber, and the escaped tear trailing down his mighty face didn't help. He opened his mouth to speak, but nothing came out but a sigh of pain that weighed heavily on his heart. Dematter stopped talking and placed two fingers on his forehead and closed his eyes as if to steady himself. Nebula stood up and tightly hugged him from behind and snuggled her head into the back of his robe as he composed himself to continue to speak.

No one knew, not even Dematter that Nebula was softly weeping. The Jungle Beauty Goddesses assumed as usual that their mother was supporting their father, who was sensitive and unafraid of showing his emotions. But appearances are not always what they seem to be, Nebula was holding on to her husband for dear life, because for the first time ever—she wished that she was capable of dying. She braced herself against his body because she knew that what her husband was about to say caused her soul to ache.

"Your mother and I arranged this dinner meeting to inform you that it is imperative that you immediately descend to planet earth to intervene on behalf of your humans in an effort to prevent their early demise. Your return to Earth is required to ward off the direst of consequences. The problem that has developed on your planet is much too grave to monitor from the Planetary Development Station. We do not know the extent of the ripple effect of damage to other planets or other galaxies for that matter that Earth has caused in the entire universe."

I am herewith providing you with Earth Laws that you must abide by for your safe return home and to prevent any further harm from being imposed upon your humans. If you fail to obey these laws, there is a chance that your mother and I may never see you again, although you cannot spiritually die, your mentality can be in such a dense form that we may possibly be unable to interact or recognize the other's being. So please listen carefully:

1. Do not engage in intimate relationships with the beings that you have created. Whenever there is a spiritual, physical, and or mental imbalance of power, one being will always exploit the other knowingly or unknowingly, and the outcome will be of a catastrophic nature.

2. I beseech you to remember always that no matter what happens—your environment and emotions will feel like reality because your spirit will be cloaked in layers upon layers of auric bodies… but never forget that it is only an illusion. In the spirit realm where we reside, there is no delay between time and space. Your thoughts are instantly visible. However when you are in dense form your spirit's ability to manifest your thoughts will be significantly suspended by the force of gravity.

3. Never use spells or magic dust to correct, intervene, or manipulate any problems or difficulties that you encounter on Earth. Earth is a planet that I designed that strictly adheres to

cause and effect laws of nature. All thoughts, actions, and behaviors shall result in physical consequences that must come to fruition because it is the basic nature of this planet.

4. The law of silence states that just because you know something, it doesn't mean that you should share it with others. Just because you have power, it does not mean that you should use it. Knowledge and silence are the pillars of wisdom. Knowledge without silence poisons the soul of its owner and everyone and everything that crosses its trail. Never tell the humans who you are, where you are from, are why you are there. Their knowledge of you will render you powerless.

5. You must forgive them ---no matter what they do to you--- no matter how horrendous, humiliating, or painful the deed is. If you don't forgive them…you will become them. There reality will become your reality. Their pain your pain. You will always remain attached to and ruled by conditions that mire your consciousness to dwelling in the past.

Return home immediately after you have discovered why Earth is disintegrating, and we will collectively develop a plan to save your planet. Are there any questions?"

"No, father," they answered simultaneously. They refused to cry or show any emotion that would cause their parents to lose faith in their ability handle this mundane matter. The Jungle Beauty Goddesses proceeded to kiss and hug both of their parents good-bye carefully avoiding any eye contact that would only intensify the moment before heading to Earth.

Kalahari was the last sister to walk out of the Chrysocolla room. Before closing the door, she turned around and said,

*"We created them; they did not create us. They are lesser beings. They have no power; we are goddesses and thou art, thou father and mother. There is nothing to worry about. We will find Afar and give her the Earth's laws before we leave. Please do not worry. We shall see you soon."*

## Chapter Six

# Tarnished Blue Ball

**Qattara's Voice**

*The trips from Ventopia to Earth was not as amusing as I had expected it to be. The mood on our spacecraft was somber and uneasy, though there was still an indomitable spirit. We barely talked at all. Unfortunately, we were unable to find Afar before leaving, but I am not worried because I am sure we will return home shortly. And as usual Afar will share some amazing tale about a faraway galaxy that she happened upon.*

*I did notice that when we passed the planet Mars, it looked desolate and cold. Maybe there is a small chance that Father was right. I don't remember there being dark, gray, smoky clouds floating around Earth when we put it back on its orbit. But I wasn't exactly paying attention that day because I was so excited about joining the star-ski competition.*

*We decided to live in our tiger's eye spacecraft underneath the sand dunes in the Namib Desert in Africa. This place has a tremendous amount of sentimental value for my sisters and I. Prior to the Deity Ball; my father named the deserts on this continent after us. I have the most horrendous feeling of foreboding in my stomach. I wonder if my sisters feel the same way. Although we are extremely polite to each other, we have avoided eye contact. I feel sick with grief. It almost feels like we are destined to live here, and home is no longer home.*

*Now that we are here on Earth, my body feels heavy and dense like a heavy, oversized garment. There are no humans in the center of the desert and my sisters, and I have all the privacy we need. We decided to go skiing on the sand dunes to relieve tension. The overflowing abundance of sand created a tunnel wave that reminded me of skiing during an anatomic expulsion of a dying star. The toasted, hot, burning, grains of sand smell like burnt sugar, which is reminiscent of home. The dry heat feels so good blowing against my face, and it reminds me of outer space where I belong. Sinai created a cascading sand fall and my sisters, and I ran through it several times before sitting under it to relax and plan our stay on Earth.*

*We decided to go to the jungle to select our favorite animal that we had created that would carry us on our journey around the entire Earth. We fed our jungle animals chi dust to make them immortal traveling companions that could expand and decrease in size as needed on our exploratory venture.*

*Namib selected a giraffe and placed a purple rose in her mouth. Sinai loved the rhinoceros because of its horrific temper that only she knew how to tame with her free spirit. The rhinoceros loved Sinai, and she loved it because they both knew that they were free, and only the journey itself was the bond that held them together. Kalahari was most proud of the magnificent stripes of the Zebra that she created and bragged about how sexy she looked riding on its back.*

*Sahara placed diamond jewels across the head of her elephant to match the jewels encircling her bald head. Chalbi loved the hippopotamus because it was aggressive, and the red fluid oozing from its pores looked like it was sweating blood. Its long, razor, sharp unending incisors gave her delicious chills each time it yawned because they reminded her of her beloved dinosaurs.*

*The horns on the African buffalo loop down before curving up like the infinity symbol without the v shape at the top. If it wore a head wrap and earrings, it would almost be as majestically beautiful as I. I created this mammal from my heart and soul, and when I jumped on top of my African buffalo my sisters gasped at how grand we looked together.*

*When my sister Afar created the leopard, she created herself in feline form. It is secretive, elusive, and shrewd and lives a solitary life. My sisters and I watched a leopard slink through the tall safari grass, pounce on its' prey, and gracefully climb up a tall tree carrying the antelope's lifeless body in its jaws. We decided to capture the leopard, place it in our spacecraft and take it back home for Afar.*

~~~

The Jungle Beauty Goddesses -- each wearing loincloths held together by chains with matching bikini tops – traveled in a caravan, from continent to continent, on the backs of their African animals. Together the six sisters screamed, “Yah!” to signal to the animals that it was time to renew the procession. The caravan walked, in a singular row, to the rhythm of the distant sound of Africa drums, snake rattles, and flutes.
~~~

Each mighty African Animal's stride was in complete sync with the others as they stepped from left to right with their heads held erect. Each animal's tail swayed from side to side in harmony with the other. Namib and her giraffe were first in line, followed by Sahara on top of her elephant, followed by Qattara straddled gracefully on top of her African Buffalo, followed by Chalbi riding on her hippopotamus, then came Kalahari on top of her Zebra, and finally Sinai, on top of her rhinoceros.

The pelvic region of each goddess appeared to be sensuously grinding up and down on the backs of their animals to the rising beat of the African drums, rattling snakes, and the moaning cries of the sad flutes as they rode off into the sunset of the African jungle to begin their journey around Earth.

If most humans could see them, they would see that the Jungle Beauty Goddesses were a smidgen taller than the tallest trees. The Goddesses could only be seen by most animals, beings visiting from other planets disguised as humans, and very few humans who had ascended their consciousness beyond time and space. But even the humans who could not actually see the Goddesses could sense their presence, upon bearing witness to unexplained phenomena such as: wind rustling through the trees, massive cracks in the cement on highways and streets, unidentifiable monstrous impressions in the earth, gigantic tidal waves, bold bright flashes of light in the night sky, and colossal bellowing thunder clouds that bawl for apparently no reason at all. Humans lacked the ability to comprehend what their senses were detecting, but they intuitively knew that earth was under observation.

The Jungle Beauty Goddesses decided that they would start their journey where it had all originally begun, near Kenya, the place where they had planted their DNA formula for humans. They expected to see humans living peacefully in tribes enjoying the plentiful lush crops of fruits and vegetables. Instead, they had front row seats to the nightmare of which they had created by being absent goddesses who left humans to fend for themselves.

They witnessed tiny, naked children who looked like skeletons covered in dark brown skin with round bellies bigger than their heads. Their empty, large bellies were filled with tragedy and hopelessness, and their sad, vacant, accusing eyes stared directly into the eyes of the Jungle Beauty Goddesses as they passed by. There were babies with flies buzzing about their heads as they suckled on the shriveled breasts of their mother's corpse.

The land looked nothing like what they had created millions of years ago. It was dirty and barren, with garbage floating down its once beautiful waters. The water drains were contaminated with human and animal feces, and the air was filled with soot. They watched humans mercilessly kill elephants and rhinoceros for their ivory. They witnessed the Earth rumble when these animals' majestic, enormous, bodies fell to the ground, leaving their orphaned calves to starve. Many animals that they had created no longer existed and were killed off for their fur, and their heads were mounted on the walls of humans.

They passed poverty-stricken areas where rich businessmen moaned in depraved ecstasy from having sexual favors performed on them by children as young as five. The parents eagerly waited to sell their children to the next customer because this was the only way they knew how to feed their families. The Jungle Beauty Goddesses marched through war zones where men, women, and children were killing each other. Dead bodies, missing limbs, beheaded corpses, burning buildings, and the wailing groans of those left behind painted an unforgettable scene that caused their souls to ache. They traveled through hauntingly beautiful, dense, dark, green forests that were filled with shallow graves of baby girls with hooded eyes and pupils as dark as a thousand midnights. Some were alive, and some were not, but they all stared at them as their caravan passed through.

Gray, dirty, smoke filled the air of some neighborhoods that were filled dilapidated buildings and homes with broken glass and trash strewn on the sidewalks. Graffiti was splashed on empty, ram shackled, gutted buildings and passageways under freeways that translated into a universal language that read: HELP! Please help us get out of here. Simultaneously, some people were dying of starvation while others left food on their plates and disposed of it; while some people turned the most beautiful beaches into their personal backyards; others shared cramped living quarters with roaches and rodents; while some worked from sun up to sun down and barely had time to tuck their babies in bed; others had servants to wash their clothes and cook their meals while they leisured about doing nothing at all.

The Jungle Beauty Goddesses felt a sense of relief as they passed through a luxurious neighborhood with sprawling trees and elegantly designed homes until a little boy, no more than 10-years-old, peered into their eyes as he held still for his sixty-year-old coach to ravish his naked bottom in unspeakable ways. In a beautiful mansion, a husband beats his wife to death with an iron rod while she begs for her life. Before she took her last breath, she locked eyes with the Jungle Beauty Goddesses and fell dead in a pool of blood that trickled over the tiny toes of her three witnessing children.

After telling grieving parents, at the funeral of their 16-year-old daughter who was killed in a drive-by shooting, how much God loved them and how this seemingly senseless death was His will, a priest walked upstairs to the 12$^{th}$ floor window of his ostentatious church steeple, took off his priest collar, looked dead into the eyes of the Jungle Beauty Goddesses, and asked, "Why did you bring us here?" He then jumped to his death.

As they traveled from continent to continent, the depth of pain and despair blurred into one; it didn't matter where they were somehow humans had managed to impoverish, pollute, annihilate, exploit and destroy planet Earth. Earth was no longer the Pretty Blue Ball that they remembered; it had now been tarnished by humans.

As long as the Jungle Beauty Goddesses remained emotionally and psychologically disconnected from Earth and all of its issues, beings, and surroundings, they would continue to be invisible to humans and thus always have access to their magnificent goddess powers. However, the massive destruction of their planet Earth was weighing heavily on their souls, and their emotions were causing them to forget who they were and why they were there. As they traveled the Earth from continent to continent, they looked at the sheer devastation that the humans had caused and wept tears that transformed into diamonds as they seeped underneath the soil.

They noticed that humans had various skin colors, hair textures, and were various shapes and sizes. Metal birds flew in the sky carrying humans from continent to continent. They drove huge metal bugs and centipedes and floated across the oceans and seas in artificial whales 100 times bigger than the real whales that the Jungle Beauty Goddesses had made. Humans ruled the land, waters, and the sky. They wondered to themselves silently how did humans develop the technology to build humongous forms of transportation and why would they have ever wanted to leave Africa and conquer the world.

The Jungle Beauty Goddesses traveled back to their spacecraft under the Namibian desert sand dunes to process everything that they had seen on planet Earth.

~~~
~~~

"We did this," Sahara said," to break the silence as the six sisters sat in a circle on top of the sand dunes. "Are humans like this because we neglected them, or did we neglect them because we are just like them? Is it possible for creations to be better than their creators?"

Qattara replied, "This is our fault. We gave them the powers of gods and goddesses when we mixed mother and father's saliva in their DNA code. We gave them bodies with undeveloped souls. We gave them brilliant minds that lack wisdom. We left them here to fend for themselves while we turned our backs on them. Look what we've done!" Qattara said while kicking a minor sand storm with one foot.

"No matter what happens, we must remain extremely calm, or we risk remaining here on Earth forever. As beings from the spiritual realm our thoughts are made of the finest, fastest light energy so we can easily manipulate, manifest, and change our perception of reality; however, the energy on Earth is vibrating at a much slower speed and once objects solidify, they are difficult to change. If we take on the feelings and emotions of the humans on Earth, we will become a part of their energy field. We must remove our sentiment from what we have observed and use logic to solve their problems and return home immediately," Sahara said matter-of-factly while blowing spiral rings of sand dust off of the palm of her hands.

"I know daddy told us not to use magic, but he would never understand the depth of destruction that has taken place on Earth. How did they transform themselves into such a variety of shapes, sizes, colors, and hair textures? They look as visibly diverse as our siblings do. We wanted them to look the same because they lacked the wisdom to handle the insignificance of perceived differences. Our time is very limited; we need to develop a plan immediately. We should cut our losses and create a chi dust elixir that alleviates all of the pain, turmoil, and suffering on Earth," Sinai said while juggling sand balls.

"I hate humans; they are the evilest, cruelest, most selfish beasts that have ever roamed this Earth. I can't believe that each one of you demanded that I agree to kill the dinosaurs to make room for such vile, wicked animals," Chalbi said. "Do you know that ninety percent of the rhinoceros population has died off because humans are killing them for their horns? I personally don't care what we do with these slimy, despicable animals. I will agree to whatever methods that will get us back home the fastest whether it is by using magic or letting them blow themselves up. Either way, I am out of here."

"Chalbi hate is an emotion too. Calm down, or else you are going to be stuck on Earth forever." Sahara warned her. "We need to think rationally and logically. We know that the ice caps are melting, which is causing the sea levels to rise, which changes the rainfall patterns that are destroying food crops and sea life-- these are not easy problems to fix. There are multiple variables that we must consider, and if we can't come to an easy solution and we are goddesses, how can we possibly expect humans to solve a problem of this magnitude?"

"It's not their fault, Chalbi," Kalahari pleads. "We were inaccessible when humans decided that they wanted to explore the globe. We don't know how many times they prayed to us or begged for our assistance. Do you know why Earth is experiencing global warming? Because we neglected them, humans decided to burn fossil fuel, which releases carbon dioxide and other gases, which traps heat in the Earth's atmosphere. Do you know what they do with this fossil fuel—they drive cars, buses. They fly planes and jets. They burn so that they can live more comfortably on Earth."

"Yes, and let's not forget that the dangerous halocarbon that humans used was to make refrigerators so that their food would not spoil; they created air conditioning so that they would be more comfortable on hot summer days. They did not use toxic halocarbons with the intention of destroying the ozone layer; their intentions are to make living conditions on planet Earth more bearable. All humans are not evil, selfish people. Many humans would have died prematurely if it were not for the medical technology that humans have created to save lives. Some humans cherish the life force that we have created for them, and they are enjoying their stay on Earth—with no assistance from us," Sinai said.

Namib added, "I think if we all calm down, we can agree that humans did not purposely destroy Earth—that was not their intent. Whatever damage they have done has been out of pure ignorance. They had no way of knowing the long-term effects of deforestation; when they cut down large number of trees to make paper, furniture, and homes, they did not understand that the carbon dioxide cycle would be disrupted. Maybe we should admit that we made a mistake by adding our parent's saliva to their DNA coding without knowing the consequences of giving them infinite potential for good and evil. We didn't want to be bothered with pesky, whining, praying, begging beings who worshipped us now. We must take responsibility for creating beings that have learned to live without the assistance of a higher power or Supreme Being. Whatever the case may be let's create a magic elixir and fix the dang-blasted problems that we have allowed to develop on Earth."

"So this is the plan," Sahara interposed, "After we mix the chi dust to correct all of the problems caused by humans, we will travel the entire world and sprinkle the magic formula over its surface. No matter what happens, remember we must remain emotionally distant from humans for us to maintain access to our goddess powers."

Qattara says, "I don't feel comfortable violating Earth's laws. Father clearly stated that we should not use magic on Earth because there must be natural consequences for cause and effect relationships."

"Look, this is not the time to become morally high and mighty. You should have taken this position prior to us adding our parent's saliva to the human's DNA code. What's done is done. We gave lesser beings powers beyond their level of spiritual maturity. If magic created the problem—then, by all means, magic can fix the problem." Sahara huffed.

"We don't know for sure that our parent's saliva caused beings to evolve in this manner in such a short period of time. This is all that I am trying to say. There may be other factors that we have not discovered yet. Daddy asked us to find out what the problems are and to report back to him so that he could help us solve them. We should at least try to figure out how and why they migrated from Africa. Maybe if we can take a moment to analyze what happened, we can come up with a better solution than sprinkling magic-fix-it chi dust over a dying planet," Qattara responded.

"I am sorry Qattara, I see your point." Sinai said, "You make a valid argument, but I say we take a vote and move forward. Time is a critical factor; planet Earth is obviously within its last days of existence if it continues to overheat at this rate. If the magic doesn't work, it could at least buy us more time to come up with a superior solution. Doing something is better than doing nothing. I'm in."

"Me too," Kalahari said. "If we had made our selves available to them, maybe they would not have resorted to such extreme measures to keep themselves intellectually stimulated. Maybe their ability to think and plan beyond the perception of reality of the present moment made them curious about future possibilities, time zones, and other life forms that urged them to explore the world. Maybe we could have helped them create an environmentally healthy way to travel the globe if we had made ourselves available to them. I love humans. I admire their tenacity. Sahara, you have my full support. What daddy doesn't know won't hurt him."

"Let's get started!" Chalbi said, "Qattara, are you on board?"

"Sure," Qattara said in a very low whisper.

~~~

The Jungle Beauty Goddesses created a magic chi dust that they placed in their pouches. They traveled the world in their caravan and sprinkled their magic chi dust that instantly improved the conditions on Earth, and every human's dream came true. The magic chi dust was a phenomenal success. It worked instantly. They were so happy with their accomplishments that before going back home to Ventopia they decided to do some research on human history to see how the humans defined and viewed themselves. They visited the International Global Gateway Library. Time appeared to stand still as the goddesses devoured every book on file.

While the Jungle Beauty Goddesses were tucked away studying the human beings that they had created from their own perspective, humans noticed that unusual, eerie events were taking place on Earth. People who were dead came back to life, and healthy people appeared to drop dead for no reason. Earth was in a state of complete chaos. Countries that did not have atomic bombs suddenly had them. Rapists, serial killers, murderers, and child molesters were released from prison. Every human's dream came true without judgment of whether it was for good or evil. Weather patterns changed radically from snow to rain to
~~~

sunshine in an instant to accommodate every human's wishes. NASA was doing everything possible to explain the unnatural events that were quickly destroying Earth.

World news reports were swamped with breaking stories of humans who had claimed to have seen a mirage of a caravan of six women traveling on jungle animals who ranged from 30 to over 150 feet tall. Witnesses described these women as having extremely long necks with decorated rings, voluptuous lips, hauntingly large eyes, and big breasts. Some eyewitnesses said that they were very ugly, creepy-looking creatures who had to have come from another planet. Others said that they looked regal, handsomely beautiful, and sad. One 12-year-old girl was interviewed on the news with a handful of diamonds that she claimed were tears from the six giant women wearing loincloths and bikini tops.

Acclaimed Paleontologist Dr. Peter L. Roy gave an interview on the world news stations stating that the descriptions of the giant women were similar to what is believed to be the first female like creature to walk the Earth. He stated that data was lacking on how this strange being lived or died, and no other skeletons of that type had been excavated. Dr. Roy reported, "We have reason to believe that these beings are armed

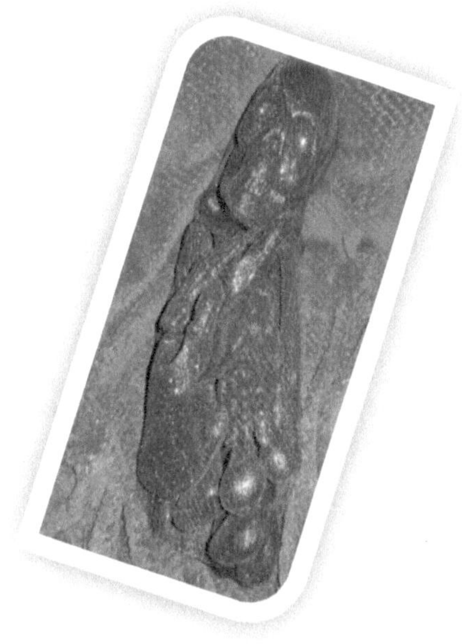

and dangerous and our international air force is on high alert. Rest assured, they will be captured."

The Jungle Beauty Goddesses spent a few days at the International Library and were totally unaware of the derogatory news reports or Earth's demise. While reading human history, they learned about the remains of human's oldest ancestor, some called her Lucy, Ardi or Eve, depending on the source. They calculated the age of the skeleton and its extremely long neck, and the sisters came to the conclusion that the skeleton was undeniably their sister Afar who neither of them had seen since they planted the humans on Earth. There were several pictures of skeleton bones with pieced together ribs, forearms, a pelvis, and one leg; even though it was all that was left of their sister—it was still their sister, and they wanted to bring her home with them where she belonged. The sisters sobbed uncontrollably at the thought of never seeing their sister again in pure form. As they wept from the depths of their soul, they forgot that their beings would become dense and visible to humans.

They read that their sister Afar's remains were in the Smithsonian museum under surveillance. They left immediately to gather what was left of her to take back home to their parents. They knew that because of the lapse in time and the missing pieces from the skeleton that even their father, Dematter, could not bring her back to life. Afar would be the first death in their family since the beginning of time.

When the Jungle Beauty Goddesses attempted to open the door of the Smithsonian Museum of Natural History, extremely loud alarms blared, with bright deep red flashing lights. Helicopters were swarming about over the building with jet planes ready to attack. Hundreds of men were lined up with machine guns pointed directly at them. A voice over a loudspeaker said, "Stop. You are under arrest. Do not move or you will be killed. Lie on the ground and put your hands behind your back." The Jungle Beauty Goddess never once thought about fighting or attacking them back in any manner because this was something that they had never experienced before. Their minds were numbed by the physical restraints of their bodies.

The Jungle Beauty Goddesses were shocked and confused and did as they were told. They could not imagine what it must feel like to be trapped or controlled by others when, throughout their entire existence they had always been free beings. The humans slapped cold, tight, handcuffs on their hands and shoved them into the back of an army truck where they were chained together with guns pointing at their heads. They were so afraid that their beings became denser and more vulnerable to human attacks. For the first time they noticed blood on their wrists where the handcuffs were too tight.

The armed guards took the Jungle Beauty Goddesses to an all-white laboratory with bright hanging lights overhead, silver cabinets, and silver metal beds with locks and chains for their hands and feet. Men with black suits, white shirts, and black ties and guns guarded every inch of the lab room. The Jungle Beauty Goddesses could not believe what was happening to them. They had never felt fear before; for the first time in their existence they felt helpless, hopeless, and powerless. They were collectively thinking to themselves how they had created humans, and it was unfathomable that they would dare hurt their creators.

The Jungle Beauty Goddesses hands and feet were chained to the metal beds. Their nude bodies were covered with a white sheet as they awaited their fate. There were three metal beds on each side of the medium size lab room. A team of human men in black pants and white lab coats came into the room to examine them. Kalahari asked them, "What are you going to do with us?" One of the human white men said, "My name is Dr. Roy, and this is my team of doctors," as he pointed to his left and then to his right. "We are not going to hurt you. We want to examine your bodies, take some specimens, and ask a few questions about where you are from and why you have come to Earth to destroy humans. You will be a little uncomfortable, but we will be as gentle as we can."

The Jungle Beauty Goddesses tried to remember that what was happening to them was not reality but an illusion based on excessive emotions. But the density of their bodies held down by gravity magnified their senses, and they felt mired to Earth's truth and not their own. Whenever they tried to forget that they were chained to metal beds, they would remember that their sister Afar's remains were locked in the Smithsonian museum. The combination of both of these issues destroyed their ability to access their goddess powers and return home.

The doctors took the white sheets off of the Jungle Beauty Goddesses and examined every inch of their nude bodies. They cringed as the cold metal instruments intruded the most intimate parts of their bodies. They felt violated in a way that they did not think was possible for any being. Kalahari was starting to cry as she looked to the side to avoid the humiliation of having doctors pinch her nipples, knead her breasts, and dig wooden sticks in her vagina held open by metal clamps. The doctors gathered around her while looking deep into her vagina with bright lights and collected fluids from her private parts that were now public—without her consent or permission. They performed the same procedures on all of the sisters who were trying desperately to control their emotions in order to escape.

"Don't cry," Qattara whispered to Kalahari. "It's not real. Control your emotions."

Kalahari tried to hold her head back as to stop the tears from running down her face. But she couldn't. Kalahari begged the doctors to please stop. But they completely ignored her. "Please stop," she pleaded to the doctors, "We have done nothing wrong." The doctors did not respond to Kalahari; they continued to probe, examine, and analyze every inch of the Jungle Beauty Goddesses nude bodies. They were very stoic and professional. When they finished gathering fluids and taking pictures of their naked bodies, Dr. Roy told them that he and his team of doctors would come back in the morning to question them.

"Then, sir will you allow us to go home?" Sahara asked as politely as she could so that she could remain calm and regain her goddess powers.

"It is very unlikely. Your species have done great damage to our planet. We must figure out why you have come to destroy us." Dr. Roy said without looking up from his writing pad.

The doctors placed the white sheets over their bodies and turned off the bright lights overhead. The red, green, blue, and yellow lights from the monitors were the only lights shining through the darkness in the laboratory room. The Jungle Beauty Goddesses heard the heavy metal doors lock behind the doctors as they left the room. One-armed male guard was left in the room who stood by the entrance metal door.

Kalahari called to the guard, "Excuse me, sir, could you please release my sisters and I? We have only come to help you, humans. You are not terrible beings. If you would just let us go we can help you get whatever you want."

The sisters begged Kalahari to distance her emotions from what was happening to them so that they could regain their powers, but she was too angry to listen.

"We made these humans. No! I will not be quiet. I have had enough of this from these lesser beings that we created by the way! He will get his ass over here and unlock these chains right now! I am his creator; he is not mine."

The security guard walked over to Kalahari, stared grimly into her eyes, and told her to shut up. Kalahari was saturated with anger that a being that she gave life to would have the audacity to talk back to her in a disrespectful manner as if they were equal beings. She spits into his face and said, "I will do no such thing. Open these chains now you insignificant speck of dust, or I will destroy you and everything you ever loved. NOW!" Kalahari growled.

Kalahari had forgotten that her anger would only decrease her strength and render her powerless. The security guard pulled the white sheet from Kalahari's body and exposed her naked body chained to the metal bed. Her fury caused her to twist, turn, and thrash about her torso to no avail. Chains around her wrists and ankles began to bleed. The security guard removed his pants and leaped onto Kalahari and began to molest her nipples and breasts with his mouth as she pleaded with him to stop. The other sisters watched in horror while at the same time trying to disconnect their emotions from what was happening to their sister, or they would never be capable of escaping.

The security guard shoved his rage inside of Kalahari's soul as she screamed and pleaded with him to stop. It seemed like her anger and fear only aroused him more, and he raped her repeatedly in front of her sisters. Although he only physically raped Kalahari, he raped the heart, mind, and soul of each sister present who was tormented by watching their sister suffer and being helpless to do anything to help her.

When he finished raping Kalahari, he tried to inject her with a serum to kill her. The other sisters realized that if they did not emotionally detach themselves immediately from humans, they would be destroyed on planet Earth. The only way that they could help the beings that they had created would be by accepting the fact that they were strangers and that they knew nothing about their way of life or what they were capable of doing. It had become painfully clear to them that just because they created humans, they did not own them nor could they control their behavior.

The security guard pulled up his pants and said to Kalahari, "I have always wanted to know what it would be like to have sex with an alien from another planet and get away with it. This is my fantasy. This is all I ever wanted. At least you kept your promise." He left the room and carefully locked the metal doors behind him.

"If you don't forgive him, we will be stuck here forever, never rescue Afar, and never see our parents again," Namib said to Kalahari.

"I hate him; I hate him, I hate him, I hate him, I hate all humans," Kalahari screamed. "Let me out of here!

"Kalahari," Sahara said, "When he raped you—he raped all of us. If you do not forgive him, you will become attached to Earth and his energy field. We could not rescue you because we were afraid. We must remember who we are. We are goddesses. We must find the mental fortitude to complete this mission with dignity."

The Jungle Beauty Goddesses chanted ohm and Tao several times to reset the vibration of their energy field to that of goddesses. The chains disappeared, and they were invisible once again. They went to the Smithsonian Museum to find Afar. When they found the shattered skeleton with missing pieces they knew it was their sister immediately by the long skeletal neck that only the Jungle Beauty Goddesses share. Only the rape could have emotionally prepared them for seeing the remains of their once immortal sister whom they loved dearly. Before the rape, the Jungle Beauty Goddesses would have cried and fallen apart upon seeing Afar's partial skeleton, but they knew that after what they had been through-- tears are a luxury for beings who have never truly had their hearts broken and their souls shattered. The Jungle Beauty Goddesses were so sad that even when they smiled it did not suit their faces.

They placed Afar's skeleton in Namib's satchel and traveled back to their spacecraft. They minimized their African animals on the spacecraft and decided to keep them as souvenirs from their journey to Earth. They closed the doors of their tiger's eye gemstone spacecraft that caused a tremendous sand storm as they took off from the Namib Desert back to Ventopia. They noticed that the further they were away from Earth, it appeared that the ozone layer was rapidly healing itself. Sahara pondered out loud, "Maybe the magic worked after all."

The ride home was solemn and quiet. There was no way of knowing if they would ever see Afar's beautiful blue eyes again, or hear the sweet sound of her voice because her being had become dense, and then fossilized into an even denser form for almost 200,000 years. The only supreme being that could possibly bring Afar back to life would be their father, Dematter—but even that wasn't certain.

## Chapter Seven

# Universal Laws

Dematter and Nebula impatiently waited for their daughters to arrive home from their trip to planet Earth. When they weren't visiting their children at the planetary development station or gliding through the various galaxies, they spent their time waltzing for hours upon hours from room to room of their spacious palace. "I have a bad feeling about this trip, Dem," Nebula whispered in her husband, Dematter's ear, as they waltzed around the grand living room to the melodic sounds of violins and piano playing from the stars. While gently rubbing her back, Dematter nuzzled his face next to hers and softly said, "There is nothing that our infinite love cannot handle. Nebula, you don't have to be strong for me. You have only trusted me completely with your smile, your joys, and your happiness. You think that I am too emotionally fragile to handle your tears, your sorrows, and your pain. But my dear, sweet, wife, you can rest thy head, rest thy heart, and rest thy faith in command of my love."

"You are making me nervous," Nebula responded, "Are you saying that you have a bad feeling too?"

"I wouldn't define it as bad. Pain and growth are usually two sides of the same coin. We can't protect our children from the pain they need to help them grow."

"I don't like this Dem. I don't like what you are not telling me. Are you keeping secrets from me? Nebula asks as she stops dancing immediately. She holds Dematter's face in both of her hands and says, "Look me in my eyes and tell me the truth; they are never coming home, are they? How will we tell Afar that her sisters are never coming home again?

Dematter wrapped his massive hands around her wrists, removed her hands from his face, and passionately kissed each hand back forth, from left to right, and then placed them around his neck; and whispered into her ear, "Shhhh dance with me love of my life." Nebula took a deep breath and allowed her being to melt into her husband's immense chest as each of their long, elegant trains of purple and black swirled about the iridescent opal floor.

While Dematter and Nebula are dancing, they hear the door to the main entrance open, but they continue dancing, assuming that it is one of their children from another galaxy dropping by to say hello simply. It never occurred to them that it could be their youngest sibling-ship, The Jungle Beauty Goddesses, arriving home from Earth. They did not hear the typical loud sounds of talking, laughter, and playfulness whenever the Goddesses were together. Ordinarily it was common to hear them before seeing them; their childlike joy always preceding them and announcing their arrival.

They danced across the floor to the main entrance door. Dematter then spun Nebula around until only a hazy swirl of dark purple clouds, made from her dress, were visible. Through the dark purple clouds Dematter saw what appeared to be his youngest daughters, except Afar, standing in the entrance. He thought to himself that it was impossible for the six girls standing in the doorway of the palace to be his daughters because of the stern, blank expressions on their faces. If indeed it were the Jungle Beauty Goddesses, they looked taller, sadder, wiser, and more regal than Dematter remembered.

The long train of Nebula's dress slowed down and blossomed into bursts of delight as she ran to greet her daughters with hugs and kisses, shouting through bouts of elation, "I never thought I would see my babies again-- but you are home at last!" She was so excited to see them that she didn't immediately notice the dismal look on their faces; that they never muttered a single word back to her; or that they did not lift their arms to hug her back--although they wanted to. The universe quivered when the swirling dagger of reality pierced into the soul of Dematter's heart and shattered the essence of his being when he realized that all seven of the Jungle Beauty Goddesses were present in one form or another. They had all changed in unexpected and unrecognizable ways to anyone who knew them prior to their visit to Earth.

Without greetings, asking questions, or even wondering why... Dematter swiftly walked over to Namib and took the satchel holding Afar's remains and hurried up the long winding spiral staircase. Nebula immediately senses that Afar is dead, and utters underneath her breath, "No, no... no...we are immortal... this is not happening," as she melts into a glob of sorrow and purple tears before fainting altogether into the loving arms of her six youngest daughters.

The Jungle Beauty Goddesses waited downstairs in the family room. A center-piece table stood on the rhodochrosite marbled gemstone floor. The room was also furnished with a white plush circular-shaped couch, covered with warm pink and soft gray pillows. As Nebula tried to sleep off the shocking news of her daughter's death, the Goddesses comforted their mother by massaging her feet, rubbing her back, and kissing her forehead. While listening to bellowing, thunderous sounds 100 times louder than a blue whale -- speaking in a language only known to a mourning soul beseeching its god – the Goddesses wondered to themselves if the god of all gods has a god. Or maybe god never needed a god because he and his loved ones were immortal—maybe until now.

In order for Dematter to bring Afar back to life he would be required to break the universal laws of gravity. These laws repel and attract order between every atom and quark, in every galaxy, on every planet, in every being, before and to the end of time. The Goddesses heard their father upstairs demanding to bring Afar back to life. They wondered whether or not universal laws are arbitrary, whimsical rules that are easily altered for supreme beings, unlike laws that strictly apply to lesser beings. Namib pondered out loud, "Are we not the only beings who want our loved ones to rise from death to life? Are we not the only beings who mourn the loss of a loved one?"

Sahara spoke softly while rubbing her mother's feet, "When our brother, Sesuj, was murdered by his beings Daddy could bring him back to life immediately because his body did not fossilize in the Lleh planet for an extended period. His being did not reach extreme levels of density, and Daddy was able to bring him back to life within three days. Afar has been on earth for hundreds of thousands of years."

Sinai sighs, "I wonder if we are only immortal because we have never found anything meaningful enough that is worth dying for. Afar took her vows. She knew what the long-term consequences would be if she deviated from them. I envy her strength."

~~~

Several flashes of blinding bright bluish-white light filled the room accompanied by the enormously loud screeching sound of a static electrical charge. Then the universe turned completely black. A dark purple thunder interstellar storm with neon fuchsia lightening was starting to brew outside. For a brief moment, time ceased to exist, and there was only the energy of nothingness and dark matter. The entire universe stood still with the exception of Dematter pacing back and forth across the window of Afar's childhood bedroom floor. He was waiting for her spiritual body to materialize from the skeleton bones underneath the sparkling black blanket.
~~~

Dematter's back was turned to Afar's bed as he stared blindly at the drifting teal puffs of stardust that fell through the dark purple storm. Even the sound of Afar softly breathing did not force him to turn around to face her. His disappointment with himself as a father, and his daughters' disobedience superseded his love at that moment, and thus he was emotionally paralyzed in sorrowfulness.

"Daddy, I love him." Afar murmured, breaking the silence that filled the room.

"You defied me." Dematter groaned.

"I was lonely, Daddy."

"Baby, you hurt me beneath the depths of my soul."

"My intentions were never to hurt you, Daddy, but to stop the aching pain in my own heart."

"I gave you everything . . . everything! I gave you a world, and even that wasn't enough. You broke your vows and made a mockery out of our kingdom and your duties as a goddess."

"Maybe it's not always about what you give Daddy… maybe what's missing are the things that you unknowingly take."

"I dare ask, what do you think I have taken from you? The entire universe has always been your playground. I have never given you interstellar boundaries that you may not cross. You have always been free to exist as you please."

"You are right. I have always been physically free, daddy. But that is no freedom at all when the price tag is conformity at all cost. You gave me powers but told me when, where, and how to use them. I had no power."

Dematter turns around from the window and walks over to Afar, and kisses her on her forehead, and sits down next to her on the bed and stares directly into her eyes and holds her cheeks in both hands and asks, "Do you think I am free? Do you think that I have the power to do any and everything that I want to do simply because I created the universe? Do you think that I am some angry, jealous, bitter, temperamental god who judges his children's deeds as good or bad and then decides who to reward or punish based on whether or not you conform to some illusionary idea of perfection? You are already

perfect because you are of me! There is nothing that I need or want from you. I am your father; you owe me nothing. I simply give you my unconditional love."

Dematter removes his hands from Afar's face, and she moves over so that he can sit next to her. "My dear, sweet child… power is restraint— just because you have it –it doesn't mean that you should use it. Do you know what it is like for me to see, hear, and know everything that is happening simultaneously and choose not to interfere with the free will of others even when I know they will be destroyed by their choices?

Do you think that I am not aware of the fact that you and your sisters infused the DNA coding of your complex beings with the saliva from your mother and me? Little did you and your sisters know that you filled your beings with the magnificent spark of their creators, and therefore you made them sleeping gods and goddesses unaware of their own powers. They are spiritual beings seeking freedom from the heavy density of their physical bodies that bound them to the gravitational weight of their planet. Your beings are destroying their planet because they feel that it is a temporary home.

The most sacred law of wisdom is silence, and the holy rule of being omnipotent is to rule with patience, compassion, and integrity. Even I am bound to the universal decree of natural consequences that one must reap what she sows and that you will always attract to you who you are. "

"Then why give us rules and laws, Daddy, when you know that we will break them."

"Because without them, there would be complete and utter chaos, everything would cease to exist and mesh into nothingness. Rules are laws that allow kindred atoms, cells, particles, ideas, beings, and objects to build, vary, and develop unlimited creations. They are not there to restrict but to refine and define an entity so that it may create a plethora of experiences, roles, and statuses for its own growth and ultimate understanding of all there is and all there could be. When universal laws are broken it simply means that there is an imbalance of wisdom and power, and the potential for growth will be temporarily suspended for all beings involved while they realign themselves with the universal laws."

"Did you know that I hated you, daddy, because I always wanted to be brown like my sisters in my sibship. I felt that you and mother loved them more because the color of their skin resembled your own. Whenever we traveled through the universe as a family I felt like I did not belong because I looked so different from everyone else. That's why I always jumped off of the train of your robe and dangled at the bottom.

I envied Sahara because she looked the most like you. I always felt like the reason that she was proud of her bald head is because her confidence and beauty emanated from knowing that she looked like her creator, father, and the person who loved her most in the universe. I never wanted to be a goddess. I always wanted my own family like you and mother, but I was never given a choice. I was born into this family with destiny and an illusion of free will."

"Other than changing your hair texture and the color of your skin to brown, what else could I have done so that you would have known how much I have and always will love you? How could I have convinced you that none of those things matter?"

"I realize now that there was nothing that you could do. It wasn't your responsibility, daddy to make me feel worthy. It was mine. You and mother treated us all the same; I needed to become my own being and search within my heart and do what was best for me. No matter how much love you and mother would bestow upon me you could never give me self-esteem or confidence in my ability. This is something that I had to earn for myself by following my dreams and disavowing my destiny. When I tell you what I have done, daddy, you will hate me forever.

"There is nothing that you can do Afar that could make me hate you because I know that at any given moment in time you are always, always doing your best based on your perception of reality. You cannot make decisions beyond your present level of consciousness. Our time together is very limited. I am open to your truth."

**Afar's Voice**

"Daddy, when we placed planet Earth back on its orbit, I decided to stay and help the human beings progress technologically. I was a little angry with my sisters for deciding to make all of the humans brown but decided to go along with the plan because I was tired of all of the bickering and fighting over developing planet Earth, and I just needed to move forward with my life.

My sisters and I created the male first in honor of you, and we named him Mada (pronounced Muh-day). The female human was programmed to emerge from the Earth a year later. We wanted to give the male an opportunity to define his masculinity before merging with female energy so that he could establish his contribution to their human existence. We thought that it would be easier for the female to feel worthy because she was endowed with the ability to bring forth life through childbirth and the choice to deviate from this role at will.

The moment I saw Mada, I fell deeply and madly in love with him. It was not the type of love that I felt for you, mother, and my siblings, but something strange and exciting that I had never felt before. I watched him hunt, fish, swim, climb, and live off the Earth. I decided to destroy the DNA coding for the female human and pursue him for myself.

One night while he was sleeping under a tree, I made myself visible and swam naked in a nearby pond. I blew a gentle breeze at the apple tree that he was sleeping under so that an apple would fall from its branch to wake him up. When he awakened and gazed at me, he jumped up and ran behind the apple tree to hide his nakedness. I noticed that he was afraid so I vanished.

I watched him sit for hours, waiting to catch fish while his stomach grumbled from hunger. I morphed into a mermaid and whistled a tune that caused an abundance of fish to swim to shore so that he could have plenty to eat. I entertained him with song and dance as I surfed the water waves hoping that he would invite me to stay. But after eating his food, he fled without acknowledging my presence or even bothering to say thank you.

Mada tried to start a fire to no avail to keep warm after bathing himself in a cool lake on a dark night. The moon highlighted his beautifully sculpted body, with tiny raised bumps that glistened over his dark brown, flawless skin, as he shivered from the cool night air. It started to rain, and his body started trembling. I defied universal laws and started a blazing fire in the pouring rain to keep him warm. I then took off my clothes, curled up next to him. I kissed, licked and massaged every inch of his perfectly chiseled body. He pretended to be asleep as I unconditionally offered all of myself to him.

The more he resisted, the more I loved him, daddy. I did everything imaginable to make him comfortable and happy, but he never wanted to so much as kiss me. I was exasperated with desire and yearning to be loved by only him, but he seemed annoyed by my presence. I offered Mada an apple as a peace offering as he sat beating his drums one evening. He politely asked me to please go away and leave him alone. I reminded him of my ingenuity and how I had given him creative ideas to help him survive and carve the most beautiful art from wood imaginable. He said that he did not need my favors to survive and if I had given him enough time he would have figured it out on his own.

We were the only two beings on the Earth, and I asked Mada if there was anything more that I could do so that he could possibly love me back. He told me that I should leave him alone so that he could discover his own strengths and weaknesses and that he was incapable of loving anyone until he had something to offer in return. He said that my gifts belittled him and made him feel small and incapable of being a self-reliant man. Mada said that the greatest gift that I could give him would be for me to go away and never speak to him again. He said that he wanted me to give him a chance to use his male prowess to pursue a woman that he loved and desired. He angrily threw the apple that I had offered him onto the ground and walked away.

I realized that I could not use my goddess powers to control his mind and his heart to make him fall in love with me, but I could use my feminine mystique to control his body against his will. One night while he was sleeping under the apple tree, I decided to tie him to it. After I tied him to the apple tree I awakened him and told him once again that I was madly and desperately in love with him and that my will would be done. I told him that we would populate the Earth with our children the way you and mother created the universe and that one day he would fall in love with me.

I told him that I would untie him if he agreed to make love to me willingly, but if he chose not to give himself to me freely then I would have no other choice than to take other measures in order to consummate my love for him.

He said that he would rather cease to exist than share his seed with a woman that he did not love and father offspring that he could not provide for. He told me that he felt like a possession instead of an equal being and begged me to let him be. He struggled to free himself from the apple tree as I pried his lips apart with my tongue. I wrapped my tongue around his tongue as he struggled to pull it away. I noticed that there was a tiny teardrop that sat on the bottom lash of each eye that he refused to let fall as I devoured his face with my kisses.

As I nibbled his earlobe, I whispered into his ear, "I will untie you if you make love to me." He tried with all of his might to make himself die, but his heart wouldn't stop beating. As I approached his lifeless manhood, he pleaded with me to stop, and offered me his next kill. I reminded him that there was nothing that he could give or do for me that I could not do for myself other than populate Earth with our children.

Although he hated me and everything that I was doing to him, his manhood was under the demand of my control. He could not stop himself from rising to the command of my feminine power and releasing his seed to me. Nor could he stop the tears that fell from each eye as he ardently screamed in ecstasy against his own will. I took his seed and mixed it with my ovule and began planting them in different regions to create people with a variety of physical traits on a continuum from his dark brown skin to my alabaster skin in various shapes and sizes over the entire Earth.

He tried to run and hide from me but I found him no matter where he went—deep in a cave, high in a tree, deep down in the valley, underneath a tunnel, or on the tip of a mountain top—each night I found him and tied him to an apple tree, and extracted his seed from his manhood by pleasuring him against his will. After the world was populated, I thought he would acknowledge the beautiful human beings that we had created together and cherished me as the Mother of Earth; but instead, he resents me.

Daddy, men all over the world, oppress women, in some way because of what I have done to Mada. I wish I had given him an opportunity to discover himself and explore his own potential before giving him technology without wisdom, and pleasure without love, and gifts without merit. Because of me, men have the illusion of freedom, but he cannot escape a woman who has decided to have her way with him, destroy his marriage, or take away his livelihood. But even with all of our feminine power, like me, women of the world are in some way single mothers and their men will never completely and naturally love them back or their children in the way that they need to be loved the most.

~ ~ ~

Afar's spiritual being was beginning to fade in and out as she was finishing her story to her father. Meanwhile, the universe was beginning to come back to life, and Nebula, and the other Jungle Beauty Goddesses heard Afar's voice and began running joyfully up the stairs to greet her.

~ ~ ~

"Daddy, I am sorry for everything that I have done. I am sorry for the pain that I have caused my sisters and this family. I am sorry for unintentionally destroying planet Earth. I realize that the freedom that I was seeking is the very freedom that I took away from Mada. Please forgive me."

"I love you, Afar. You will always be daddy's little girl, and I will always love you. I broke all of the universal laws for this brief moment in time because I needed to bring you back home one last time to say goodbye…because I will never lay eyes upon you again…"

Tears stream down Dematter's face as he tells Afar, I need you to know without a single doubt that your daddy has always… and will always love you no matter what you do or who you love. You are incapable of ever stopping me from loving you. I am proud of you, and without reservations, I know that you and your sisters will find a way to save planet Earth. Your spirit is now intertwined with the energy force of Earth and its beings, and you can never return home to Ventopia."

"I know daddy," Afar whispered underneath the tears flowing down her face. She looked at her father tenderly, while her heart took a picture of the last moment in time that she would ever see him again. "Will you tell mother that I love her? I will miss the manna muffins and lavender tea, sitting with my sisters under the pink ponytail trees. I will miss gliding through the universe with you and my sisters…" Afar's spiritual presence begins to fade further away.

Dematter hugs Afar's fragile, dissipating being and tells her, "Earth will now be esteemed and protected the way it was intended to be. You are Mother Earth, precious child. You did a brave thing, Afar; you followed your heart … you fell in love. No one can blame you for falling in love."

"Daddy, will Mada ever love me back?" She muttered before completely turning back into a skeleton.

Dematter hugs Afar as she dissolves in his arms and returns to the skeleton bones lying on the bed. When Nebula arrives to the room she catches a quick glimpse of her daughter right before her spiritual being disappears completely. She runs to the bed, picks up Afar's skeleton and begins sobbing, "No, no, no, bring her back! Please, please bring back my baby. Take me instead if you must … please, please, please bring back my baby!"

Dematter hugs his wife and tries to console her while she holds Afar's remains against her chest. Nebula sobs into her husband's arms, "Bring her back, Dem. Bring her back for me. If you love me, you will bring her back!" By this time the six Jungle Beauty Goddesses have arrived in the room. They formed a circle around their parents and hugged them without so much as shedding a single tear.

He gently removed Afar's remains from his wife's clutched arms and placed them back into the satchel and gave it to Namib. Dematter made an effort to sound calm as he said, "You and your sisters must return to planet Earth and bury Afar's skeleton into the desert where she belongs. While she is away from Earth, the ozone layer is beginning to heal itself, and global warming is going into remission. The industrial and technological advances that humans made under Afar's guidance are vanishing from the planet. Although the Earth atmosphere is being ecologically healed, humans are regressing to a less complex, simpler society and dying from diseases, illnesses, and accidents that had been cured centuries ago. You are to remain with your sister on Earth until its life forms are no longer in danger of premature extinction and you have bridged the gap between knowledge, wisdom, and technological progress."

The Jungle Beauty Goddesses assured their father that they would return Afar safely back to Earth. They kissed the back of their mother's head. Nebula was distraught in grief as her entire being was meshed into their father's arms. He promised them that he would take care of their mother and told them that he was confident in their ability to save planet Earth.

While on their spacecraft headed back to the Pretty Blue Ball, planet Earth the sisters placed their hands on the satchel containing Afar's skeleton and said together, "I love you sister. One as the same, the same as one-- without you- there would be none."

After their tribute to Afar, each sister walked to their private quarters on the spacecraft. Sinai noticed that Kalahari had a strange glow about her and asked her if she was feeling okay. Kalahari confided to Sinai that she felt a strange queasy feeling in her stomach that she had never felt before. Sinai told her that it was only the fear of the unknown that was causing her stomach to quiver. "We don't know if we will ever see Afar again or be able to save planet Earth. You are lucky that all you have is a little tummy ache," Sinai said as she playfully rubbed her belly, kissed her forehead, and settled into her quarters for the ride back to Earth.

***~To Be Continued…~***

www.ingramcontent.com/pod-product-compliance
Lightning Source LLC
LaVergne TN
LVHW041040150826
845672LV00001B/399

* 9 7 8 1 7 0 7 0 6 4 2 8 1 *